Analise had always known what she'd wanted.

Until this trip.

Until she met Nick.

Suddenly everything around her was confusing and complicated and her wants were contradictory. She wanted to make her parents happy, stop their worrying about her, and she could do that by marrying her fiancé, Lucas.

That would make her happy, too, of course.

All she had to do was stay away from Nick, not touch him, not look at him, not think about him, not dream about him at night.

She could do that.

She *had* to do that.

Dear Reader,

The wonder of a Silhouette Romance is that it can touch *every* woman's heart. Check out this month's offerings—and prepare to be swept away!

A woman wild about kids winds up tutoring a single dad in the art of parenthood in *Babies, Rattles and Cribs... Oh, My!* It's this month's BUNDLES OF JOY title from Leanna Wilson. When a Cinderella-esque waitress—complete with wicked stepfamily!—finds herself in danger, she hires a bodyguard whose idea of protection means making her his *Glass Slipper Bride,* another unforgettable tale from Arlene James. Pair one highly independent woman and one overly protective lawman and what do you have? The prelude to *The Marriage Beat,* Doreen Roberts's sparkling new Romance with a HE'S MY HERO cop.

WRANGLERS & LACE is a theme-based promotion highlighting classic Western stories. July's offering, Cathleen Galitz's *Wyoming Born & Bred,* features an ex-rodeo champion bent on reclaiming his family's homestead who instead discovers that home is with the stubborn new owner...and her three charming children! A long-lost twin, a runaway bride...and *A Gift for the Groom*—don't miss this conclusion to Sally Carleen's delightful duo ON THE WAY TO A WEDDING.... And a man-shy single mom takes a chance and follows *The Way to a Cowboy's Heart* in this emotional heart-tugger from rising star Teresa Southwick.

Enjoy this month's selections, and make sure to drop me a line about *why* you keep coming back to Romance. We want to fulfill *your* dreams!

Happy reading,

Mary-Theresa Hussey

Mary-Theresa Hussey
Senior Editor, Silhouette Romance
300 East 42nd Street, 6th Floor
New York, NY 10017

Please address questions and book requests to:
Silhouette Reader Service
U.S.: 3010 Walden Ave., P.O. Box 1325, Buffalo, NY 14269
Canadian: P.O. Box 609, Fort Erie, Ont. L2A 5X3

A GIFT FOR THE GROOM

Sally Carleen

Silhouette

V™ R O M A N C E™

Published by Silhouette Books

America's Publisher of Contemporary Romance

To Paula Stewart, my "blood sister"
and sister of the heart

 SILHOUETTE BOOKS

ISBN 0-373-19382-3

A GIFT FOR THE GROOM

Copyright © 1999 by Sally B. Steward

This edition published by arrangement with Harlequin Books S.A.

Visit us at www.romance.net

Printed in U.S.A.

Books by Sally Carleen

SALLY CARLEEN,

the daughter of a cowboy and a mail-order bride, has romance in her genes. Factor in the grandfather in 1890s Louisiana who stole the crowd at political rallies by standing on a flatbed wagon and telling stories, and it's no surprise she ended up writing romance novels.

Sally, a hard-core romantic who expects life and novels to have happy endings, is married to Max Steward, and they live in Missouri with their large cat, Leo, and their very small dog, Cricket. Her hobbies are drinking Coca-Cola and eating chocolate, especially Ben & Jerry's Phish Food ice cream. Sally loves to hear from her readers. You can write to her c/o P.O. Box 6614, Lee's Summit, MO 64064.

OKLAHOMA

NEW MEXICO

ARK.

Dallas •

Tyler •

Briar Creek

LA.

TEXAS

★ Austin

N

MEXICO

Gulf of Mexico

All underlined places are fictitious.

Chapter One

The bottom half of the scorching sun had disappeared behind the distant mountains when Nick Claiborne strode across the tarmac of the small airport in Rattlesnake Corners, Wyoming. His V-tail plane, N373GY, affectionately known as Ginny, sat waiting patiently for his return.

The June day had been long and hot. He'd left South Dakota early that morning, flown to Wyoming, spent the day looking for a woman who'd moved over twenty years ago, and now he had to fly to Nebraska tonight in search of that same woman.

Once he and Ginny got into the air, free of the earth, up there alone with the stars, he'd unwind and relax. It was always like that when he could find the time to fly. As a private investigator, he didn't get to do a lot of flying. This case, frustrating in many ways, at least gave him the excuse to travel.

He completed his preflight walk-around check, unfastened Ginny's tiedowns and climbed up the wing to the door, which stood slightly open. That was odd. He was always so careful to lock it.

He swung the door wide open, preparing to climb in, to settle in the seat that, after so many hours of use, molded to his body perfectly. Already he could feel the tension unknotting in his neck and shoulders as he caught the familiar scent of...no, something was wrong. His plane wasn't supposed to smell like honeysuckle.

"Hi! I'm Analise Brewster! You must be Nick Claiborne."

Nick blinked and dropped his foot back to the wing. He wasn't given to hallucinations, hadn't drunk anything all day except water and iced tea and he was pretty sure he wasn't asleep and dreaming. Therefore, the redhead in his cockpit must be real.

"Analise Brewster?" he repeated. "My client Analise Brewster?" As if there could be more than one.

"That's right! Am I glad to see you! It's getting so late, I was starting to worry, afraid I'd been waiting in the wrong plane, except this is the only plane parked here."

She swung out slender feet in turquoise sandals followed by long, golden legs stretching at least a mile from khaki shorts that should have been mundane and ordinary but somehow on this woman were incredibly sexy. She wore some kind of silky, turquoise blouse that draped oh so nicely over her rounded breasts.

He made himself lift his gaze to her face.

Standing in front of him, almost even with his height of six feet, due to the upward slope of the wing where she stood, she smiled tentatively, her lush, generous lips outlining white, perfect teeth.

Lush, generous lips? Where the hell had that come from?

Okay, maybe they were lush and generous, but he didn't need to be thinking that about some woman who'd ambushed him from his own plane...some engaged woman.

She extended a slim hand, and he accepted automatically,

too stunned to do otherwise, his fingers closing over the smooth skin.

"In your fax," she said, "you mentioned that you thought you had a solid lead on Abbie Prather. Did you find her today? Is she in jail already?"

Maybe one of those ranchers had slipped something into that iced tea after all. This whole scene didn't bear much resemblance to reality. He rubbed the back of his neck where those tension knots were gathering again. "What are you doing here? How did you get into my plane?"

"I got your fax last night," she explained, speaking more slowly, as if she thought he might have difficulty comprehending. She was right about that! "Then I called your office this morning and told your secretary that I planned to meet you here, but I guess you didn't get my message."

"No, I didn't get your message. I haven't talked to my office today." Nick looked around the deserted airport. "How did you get here?"

"I drove to Tyler this morning and rented a plane—we don't have an airport in Briar Creek—and when I got here, you weren't here, but that man inside told me this was your plane and you'd be back since you'd borrowed his truck because there weren't any rental cars, so I, um, sort of waited. In your plane. So I wouldn't miss you."

She was once again talking even faster than he remembered from their phone conversations. But the wires and circuits of the phone lines hadn't done justice to that voice. Even in fast forward it called up images of cool lemonade sipped under the shade of a big cottonwood tree in the heat of a Texas summer, of warm breezes sifting through the smooth leaves of a magnolia tree.

He cleared his throat and tried to do the same with his mind. "I still don't understand what you're doing here."

For a brief moment confusion creased her smooth forehead. She looked around as if a little surprised to find herself in the middle of nowhere. Then her gaze returned to him and her smile re-formed. "Why, to be there when you find the woman who framed my fiancé's father, of course."

He folded his arms across his chest. "Why?"

"Why?" Again she looked a little uncertain. "Well, I should think that would be obvious."

"It's not, so why don't you enlighten me? What possible reason could you have for traveling a thousand miles just to see some woman arrested?"

She bit her lower lip, and Nick found himself unconsciously imitating her action, chewing on his own lip as if he could taste hers by proxy. This woman was dangerous.

She twisted around, bent over and reached into the plane. He tried not to look at her rounded rear in those mundane khaki shorts. Tried and failed.

She straightened and hauled out a satchel that was either a very large purse or a small suitcase. From the bag, after some searching, she produced a camera. "I could take a picture," she said. "As I already explained, hiring you to find that woman is a wedding present for Lucas. That's my fiancé. But I haven't told him yet since it's a surprise, so I could take a picture as sort of physical evidence. Something to put under the tree, so to speak. Not that we're having a tree at our wedding. But you know what I mean."

"No," he said. "I don't know what you mean. You just now made that up about taking the picture. You still haven't told me why you're here."

She plunked the camera back into her bag, slung it over her shoulder, lifted her chin defiantly and met his gaze head-on. "I need to be here."

Her eyes were decidedly green, even in the deepening dusk. Not blue-green like the ocean or gray-green like moss, but green like the treetops in full summer when he flew above them. An urge swept over him to dive into their depths, to assure her it didn't matter why she'd come to him, that he was glad she was there.

He gave himself a mental shake. It wasn't like him to let his hormones take over so completely. He was upset she was there, not glad.

"Abbie Prather's not here," he growled, irritated with himself as much as with her. "She moved in 1976."

"Oh, no! You mean we've lost her? What are we going to do now?"

She looked so forlorn, he had to fight a totally irrational desire to reassure her, to try to make things right...to take care of her.

Been there, done that, he reminded himself grimly.

He was a private investigator, his services for hire. Gather information, get the facts. That was what he did, and all he did. No involvement with anybody's problems.

"We—*I* haven't lost her. I've got a new address for her in Nebraska. I'm flying there tonight just as soon as you get back in your chartered plane and return to Briar Creek."

"Ah, well, you see," she began, looking over his left shoulder, refusing to meet his gaze, "that's not exactly possible. My pilot had to turn around and fly back because today's his son's sixth birthday, and they're having a party for him right about now, so I'll just go on to Nebraska with you and then maybe I'll be there when you find Abbie after all."

"You can't do that!" Nick protested, a jumbled panic prickling him from all sides. He needed his downtime, his time alone. He did not need a ditzy client hanging around...especially not a ditzy client with golden legs nine miles long and lush lips.

"Why not?" she asked.

"Look, Ms. Brewster—"

"Analise. We should certainly be on a first name basis if we're going to Nebraska together in that itty-bitty plane."

"We're not going to Nebraska together in that itty-bitty…in my plane. Or anybody's plane." Nick plowed his fingers through his hair and shook his head. "Abbie Prather is no amateur. She stole twenty-five thousand dollars from the bank where she worked, manipulated bank records to frame your fiancé's father then obtained documentation to change her identity to June Martin. These are the actions of somebody who knows how to play the game. Now you figure she ran to South Dakota, lived there a couple of years and moved to Wyoming, lived here a couple of years and moved to Nebraska. What makes you think she stayed in Nebraska more than a couple of years? She probably moved another six or seven times. I told you when I took this case that it was going to be tough because it's so old."

Analise folded her arms, right under her rounded breasts, pushing them up, thrusting them forward, pulling the smooth turquoise silk taut over them, emphasizing every curve. He'd thought the summer evening was cooling off, but that was before Analise folded her arms under her breasts.

"There's no motel or car-rental place closer than Casper," she said firmly. "The man inside told me that. There used to be a motel in Thunder Bluffs, but it burned to the ground when lightning struck it four years ago, or maybe it was five, depending on whether you believe him or the cowboy who came in while I was there. So unless you plan to make me spend the night out here on this hard, cold ground where there are probably rattlesnakes—why else would they call this place Rattlesnake Corners?—you'll have to take me to Nebraska."

With a sinking feeling, Nick realized she was right. His plans for a peaceful, restorative, solitary trip fluttered away into the night. At the moment he had no choice. He lifted his hands in resignation. "All right, all right! I'll take you to Nebraska and tomorrow morning you'll make arrangements to get home."

"Okay."

"You're *not* going with me traipsing around the countryside looking for Abbie Prather."

"I said okay. What's your problem?"

He wasn't sure he believed her. He was both dreading and looking forward to flying to Nebraska with her in that itty-bitty plane. Those were his problems.

"As long as we understand that you're not going to be present when I find Abbie Prather."

She didn't say anything.

"That's the job you hired me to do. If you hire somebody to paint your house, do you insist on taking up a brush and helping him?"

"I live with my parents. They're the ones who hired that painter. He had a fear of heights and our house has three stories and sits on top of a hill besides. So of course I helped him."

Somehow her answer didn't surprise him.

"Well, you're not going with me tomorrow, and that's that." He climbed into the cockpit and slid into his familiar seat. But it seemed to have developed new contours and no longer fit him so well, as if Analise's intrusion into his haven had altered it physically.

She got in beside him and closed the door. Odd that he'd never before noticed how small this cabin was, how close his seat was to the passenger's.

He fastened his seat belt and focused on his starting checklist, making a concerted effort to ignore his passenger.

Just as the engine growled to life, Analise pulled a bag of chips out of that huge purse of hers, ripped them open and began to crunch.

"Could you keep it down? You're making more noise than the engine."

"Sorry. Flying makes me nervous, so I eat to distract myself."

Oh, great! "Do you have a candy bar in there or something a little quieter?"

She stuffed the chips back into her purse. "I hope you're not going to be this cranky the whole way to Nebraska."

"I am," he assured her. "In fact, it's probably going to get worse. By the way, you never did tell me how you got into my plane. I know I left the door locked."

She peeled the wrapper off a candy bar. "Picked the lock. I learned how to do it in college."

"You learned to pick locks in college? Where did you go? Burglar U?"

She lifted an eyebrow at his absurd question. "I went to school in Austin. I dated a guy who taught me to pick locks, among other things."

"Other things?" He wasn't sure he wanted to hear those other things, but he couldn't stop himself from asking.

"We ran together, five miles a day. Physical fitness. Then there was scaling six-foot fences, playing poker and blackjack, dealing off the bottom of the deck, shooting a .38 revolver—"

"Shooting a—you dated a criminal?"

"Of course not! Richard was an undercover cop. Would you like a candy bar? I have plenty."

"No, thank you," he muttered. His neck muscles had tied themselves into tight knots again, and he could feel a headache building behind his eyes.

He tried to focus on the things he loved about flying, especially flying at night—the sense of freedom, of isolation and serenity. For the next hundred or so miles, the land below would be totally dark except for the occasional car or house. No city lights. Nothing around anywhere...north, south, east, west, up or down.

Nothing but Analise Brewster with her lush, generous

lips wrapped around a candy bar, her long legs tucked demurely to one side and looking anything but demure. Analise Brewster sitting inches away from him, touching him with the combined, oddly compelling scents of honeysuckle and chocolate.

"Put your legs down and fasten your seat belt," he barked.

She complied so hastily he felt a little guilty for snapping at her.

He taxied to the run-up area and went through his instrument check then took up the microphone to announce his intention to take off to any planes that might be within radio range.

This was going to be a long, long flight.

Analise took a large, desperate bite out of her candy bar as she felt the plane lift off the ground, and her stomach gave a corresponding lurch right into her throat. This was the scariest and most exciting part of flying, that moment of actually going up into the air, unsupported by anything but magic. She understood how butterflies flew and how it was impossible for bumblebees to fly even though they did. But the unlikelihood of a bumblebee's flight didn't even come close to the impossibility that tons of metal with wings that couldn't flap should be able to stay aloft.

She ate more of her candy bar, ignored those butterflies that had taken up residence in her lurching stomach and resisted the urge to chatter, something she was prone to do when she was nervous. Nick had indicated he needed silence while he got everything going and she certainly didn't want to cause him to do something wrong, something that would break the magic spell and send them plummeting to earth.

She'd done enough chattering tonight, anyway. By the time he'd arrived, she'd been pretty nervous, had begun to think she was going to have to spend the night in the plane. In fact, from the time she'd walked into the airport, her rented plane already on its way back to Tyler, only to find that Nick wasn't waiting for her, she'd been getting progressively more concerned.

This latest impulsive act, charging across the country a week before her wedding, might not prove to be one of her better ideas. In fact, it would probably go down in the column of incidents that reinforced her parents' incessant worries about her. It seemed the harder she tried to be the perfect daughter, the worse things got.

Her parents weren't happy that she'd taken so long to make up her mind about marrying Lucas Daniels. Their wedding was wedged in next Saturday between morning and evening ceremonies and their rehearsal was scheduled for today, a week early, the only time they could get the church.

And the closer it got to that rehearsal, the edgier and more claustrophobic she got. Somewhere around four o'clock this morning, she'd decided that what she really needed to do was come to Wyoming to be certain Nick was able to garner enough evidence to clear Lucas's father's name before the wedding so his parents would come. Her concern over that issue had doubtless been causing her distress.

It had seemed like such a good idea at the time, but now Nick's pointed questions made her wonder about her motivation. It wasn't exactly logical.

One foul-up after another. The story of her well-intentioned, ill-fated life.

As she desperately devoured her candy bar, she stole a glance at Nick. The shadowy, uneven light from the instrument panel accented the craggy planes of his face, giving him an even more intriguing, dangerous look than when she'd first met him. His shaggy brown hair, just a little too long, touched the collar of his faded denim shirt. The top buttons of that shirt were undone, allowing springy tufts of that same hair to escape.

She twisted the diamond ring on her finger and thought of how lucky she was to be engaged to a nice man like Lucas Daniels. She pictured his handsome face with his kind smile, his immaculately cut and styled black hair that told of his Native American heritage. Lucas was her best friend, her parents' best friend. When she and Lucas were married, her parents would finally have to admit that she'd done something right. They could stop worrying about her every minute of every day.

She was glad she'd made the last-minute decision to marry him. This antsy, trapped feeling was probably normal for a bride-to-be.

In six and a half days she'd marry Lucas and that would at least keep her out of one brand of trouble. Never again would she run the risk of becoming involved with a man because he had that aura of danger and defiance.

The aura Nick exuded from every pore.

He set the automatic pilot and leaned back.

Analise crumpled the empty candy-bar wrapper and pulled out a bag of chocolate sandwich cookies.

"No wonder you're so hyper, eating all that sugar," Nick grumbled.

"I told you, flying makes me nervous."

"Why do you fly if it makes you nervous?"

"Because it's the fastest way to get places, of course. Anyway, I have a theory. If you're afraid of something, you have to do it and then you won't be afraid of it. Since my parents have made a career out of worrying about me, I could be afraid of everything if I didn't make an effort to do all the things they think I shouldn't do." She offered him the bag of cookies. "Here. You could stand to relax a little, too. Surely you're not nervous about flying. Although, if you go along with my theory, becoming a pilot would be the logical thing to do to overcome that fear.''

"I love to fly." He accepted a couple of cookies. "But I didn't have any dinner.''

That was a good sign. Eating cookies together was always a bonding experience.

"So," she said brightly, hoping to inspire a bit of brightness in her cranky pilot, "tell me what you discovered today about Abbie Prather." He didn't respond immediately. His jaw muscle twitched. Maybe he was still chewing on that cookie. "You can just give me your report verbally instead of faxing it to me since I'm not home to receive the fax," she encouraged, giving him plenty of time to swallow.

His lips compressed as if the cookie tasted bad or he didn't want to comply with anything she asked. She knew there was nothing wrong with the cookie.

"I searched the records in Casper," he finally said, "and talked to people who live in the area where Abbie Prather lived, and I found out two things. She moved to Nebraska in about 1976, and she had a little girl with her.''

Analise stopped with her cookie halfway to her mouth. "A little girl? Where did she get a little girl?"

"I would imagine she got her in the usual way.''

"But she didn't have a baby when she left Briar Creek! And you didn't mention any baby in South Dakota, or any husband!''

"No evidence of a husband. My guess would be that she either had the child right before or right after she left Texas. The people I talked to today figured the kid to be about two when she moved here and four when she left.''

"But where was this baby when she was in South Dakota?''

"In South Dakota she lived out away from people, just like she did in Wyoming. If she'd had a baby with her in

South Dakota, it would have been easy to hide her. A toddler's another story, and the people who saw this little girl said she was a pistol. Very visible. Had red hair and was always getting into something. Every time they saw her, the kid was charging around and Abbie was yelling at her, though they said by the time she left, the kid was getting kind of cowed by all that yelling."

Analise touched her own curls, sadness sweeping over her at the thought of Abbie's daughter being cowed. "A little red-haired girl, four years old. She'd be about my age. If Abbie hadn't stolen that money and left town, her daughter and I might have been friends. That's terrible that Abbie yelled so much at her that she broke her spirit. But at least now we know why she stole the money."

"You think stealing the money to take care of her kid justifies her actions?"

"No, of course not! But it explains why she did it. She must have been pregnant in Briar Creek and the father wouldn't marry her so she had to leave in shame—"

"*Leave in shame?* This was 1972, not 1872."

"Briar Creek can be pretty provincial. Anyway, she managed to hide her pregnancy, but she knew she couldn't hide the baby…they make too much noise…so she stole the money and left town. If she'd stayed in Briar Creek and given her child up for adoption, my parents might have taken her and I'd have had a sister. They wanted another child."

The idea brought an eerie sense of déjà vu, doubtless because she'd always wanted a sister, had even invented one when she was a child, a red-haired sister who looked like her and was named Sara. How sad that she'd missed the possibility. Sad for her and the other little girl. Abbie didn't sound like an ideal mother, while her own parents were practically perfect…unlike their changeling daughter.

"That's pretty much the way I had it figured," Nick said.

"However, you should realize that this could mean your fiancé's father was the father of her baby."

"No way!"

"Then why did she choose him to take the blame?"

"Because he was the most likely candidate. He'd been in trouble before when he was a teenager. His family was really poor, and when he was in high school he was dating Lucas's mother, whose family wasn't poor though they weren't wealthy, either. Anyway, he wanted to take her to his senior prom but he couldn't afford to rent a tuxedo, so he stole one. At least, he tried to steal one. They caught him. He got off with probation because he'd planned to return it after the prom and he was an honor student and he'd never been in any kind of trouble before, but when that thing at the bank came up and he looked guilty, nobody bothered to check any further."

"Which doesn't mean the man wasn't the father of Abbie Prather's child. Why didn't your fiancé look into this?" He lifted a hand to cut off her protestations. "I just think you ought to know that you may be opening a can of worms here. This may not be the kind of wedding present your Lucas wants. There may be a good reason he never investigated."

"There certainly is a good reason. Well, a fairly good reason. It's real good if you understand Lucas's point of view. He was only four years old when his dad was convicted, so pretty much all he remembers is how people treated the family of a convicted felon. As soon as his dad got out of prison sixteen years ago, they moved to Pennsylvania where nobody knew anything and started over. His parents have told him repeatedly that they have to forget the whole thing, move forward and put it behind them. Give themselves and everybody else a chance to forget. They won't even come back to Briar Creek for our wedding."

"If they don't want to dredge the whole thing up, why are you doing it?"

"So his parents can feel comfortable coming to our wedding and because Lucas really does want to know the truth, deep inside."

"I see." Disbelief oozed from the pores of both words.

"He does! Okay, he's never really said it in so many words, but he says it every day by his actions. He's a doctor. He could practice anywhere in the country, but he chose to move back to Briar Creek and go into practice with my dad. He tries really, really hard to be an exemplary citizen and show people by the way he lives that his father couldn't possibly be guilty. If he says his dad's a total straight-arrow, I believe him. You find that little girl's birth certificate and we'll see who the father is and I guarantee it won't be Wayne Daniels."

"I fully intend to do that, but this is Saturday night, and the courthouses won't be open until Monday morning at nine."

She sighed. "Then I guess we'll have to wait to settle that point. What's the little girl's name? Did anybody remember?"

"Oh, yes. Several people remembered because Abbie yelled at her so much, calling her name. It's Sara."

Talk about déjà vu! "Sara," she repeated. "When I was a little kid, my imaginary sister's name was Sara, and then I gave the name to my favorite doll when I was six."

"It's a common name."

"I guess so." But her doll, like her and like Abbie's daughter, had red hair. In fact, she still had the doll in a carriage in one corner of her room, a part of her childhood she couldn't seem to let go of.

She sat quietly for a moment, thinking about Abbie's daughter and the coincidences of their similarity in hair color and age and of having a doll with the girl's name. If she believed in fate, she'd have thought Sara was destined to be her friend or even her adopted sister, and Abbie's crime had sent fate awry.

Many times she'd overheard her parents lament that she had no sister and talk tentatively about having another baby. When she was young, she'd believed they'd refrained from having one because she was such a problem, they didn't have enough worry left over for a second child. Now that she knew more about the process of obtaining babies, she realized perhaps they hadn't been able to have another.

Or it could be that her original assumption was right. In her zeal to prove she was competent, she usually ended up proving the opposite. Like with this trip.

The plane hit an air pocket, bouncing down and startling her, throwing her forward. Though her seat belt held her securely, Nick swung an arm across her, the way her parents had done when she was a child riding in the car and they'd had to stop suddenly.

But Nick's touch didn't feel paternal as his arm pushed against her left breast, his flattened palm against her right. Her gaze darted to the side, to look at him, without turning even her head as if the slightest movement would increase the accidental, forbidden, delicious sensations of his touch. And the horrible part was, she wanted to increase those sensations, to push them to their limits, whatever those limits might be.

She bit her lip. She shouldn't be having those thoughts while she was engaged to Lucas! Talk about limits—she'd gone over the line already!

And she'd thought getting out of Briar Creek for a while would help her relax! She should have gone to one of those South American countries where they had the Revolution of the Week. That would have been more tranquil than flying to Nebraska with Nick Claiborne.

He was leaning forward, staring at her, and for a moment

frozen in time, neither of them moved. His eyes which had been the color of the Texas sky at daybreak when she'd first seen him were now dark like the sky as a storm rolled in, dark from leashed energy and power ready to explode over the land in a wild tempest.

An illusion because of the dim light in the plane, she told herself.

But logic didn't alter the effect of his gaze, the storm his touch created in her.

As if he'd suddenly noticed where it was, he jerked his hand back to his side and turned toward the front of the plane, to the darkness outside. "Sorry," he said, his voice strangely husky. "Automatic reflex. I had four little sisters and an ex-wife who refused to wear her seat belt in the car or the plane."

She swallowed hard. "No problem. I understand."

She plowed into her handbag and brought out the rest of the cookies then crammed a whole one into her mouth. If eating could distract her from her fear of flying, surely it could distract her from the pilot, from the memory of his hand on her breast, from the tingling, tantalizing sensations that still lingered where he'd touched her and from the guilt of betraying Lucas, her best friend.

He leaned forward and made an adjustment of some sort. His movement stirred the air in the small space, releasing a scent of dusty denim and dangerous, tantalizing masculinity that she'd have recognized anywhere as belonging to Nick.

Only half a bag of cookies, three more candy bars, two packages of chips, a roll of mints and a bag of pistachio nuts remained in her purse. It probably wasn't going to be enough.

Chapter Two

Nick awoke to the groaning of water pipes. At least he hoped it was water pipes. Otherwise, somebody was being tortured in a nearby room of the Rest-a-While Motel in Prairieview, Nebraska.

He could only hope Analise Brewster had slept half as badly as he had. If she had, she'd surely be ready to go home.

When they'd arrived in the middle of the night, the outside temperature had been cool, but inside the tiny room was another matter. He'd fully expected someone to come in just before dawn and shove in a few loaves of bread to bake. The sleepy owner they'd rousted out of bed had apologized for the fact that the air-conditioning was broken. Nick had his doubts that the place had ever possessed such a modern convenience.

To make matters worse, he'd had no dinner the night before except the cookies Analise had given him. Every thought of the room's being hot enough to bake bread, fry eggs, boil soup, had been related to food and had sent his stomach into growling frenzies.

However, neither the heat nor his hunger had been the primary reason he'd tossed and turned all night, kicking the sheet into a twisted rope at the end of the lumpy bed.

Analise had been the primary cause of his disquiet. Analise, who'd talked and snacked pretty much the entire trip, including the drive from the small airport to Prairieview in the rattletrap rental car his contact had left for him. She'd talked about her fiancé, his father, his mother, her mother, her father, her friends… She'd filled his plane with so many people, making them so real, he'd halfway expected them to walk out of the plane when they landed.

By the time they arrived at the motel, the last two years of peace and tranquillity had disappeared without a trace and he was back in chaos. He'd grown up with four—count 'em, *four*—little sisters who'd kept the pandemonium at a consistently high level and regularly dived headfirst into situations from which he had to rescue them. Then, like a man possessed by masochism, when his twin sisters left for college, he'd married a ditzy woman who made his sisters seem staid and reasonable. His twin sisters had left three years ago and the ex-wife four months after he'd married her. Two years of serenity…until last night. Until Analise.

She was like his sisters and his ex-wife all put together then multiplied. And to make it worse, his hormones didn't care. They would betray him, sell him down the river, send him into servitude just to have Analise. He wasn't sure how it was possible, but while his brain told him to get away and save himself while he still could, his body wanted her with an intensity that threatened to overrule his brain.

What little sleep he'd caught in fleeting snatches had been filled with dreams of Analise…Analise talking, eating, offering him candy, taking candy from his fingers with those soft, full lips—

A knock on the door interrupted the thoughts Nick didn't want to be having but couldn't seem to stop. He untwisted the sheet from his ankle, retrieved his blue jeans from the worn carpet and went to answer the door.

In the harsh glare of morning sunlight, Nick hallucinated a short, rounded angel with a wrinkled, cherubic face and a halo of snow-white curls. She wore a navy blue dress with white lace on the collar just like the one his grandmother had worn for church and funerals. She beamed up at him and shoved a large tray toward him. "Good morning, Mr. Claiborne. I brought you some breakfast."

He blinked a couple of times but the hallucination didn't go away. In fact, his nose was getting in on the act now, telling him the angel carried bacon, eggs and coffee on that tray.

He stepped back, allowing the angel to enter his room. With any sort of luck, he could get a few bites of those eggs and a couple of sips of coffee before the hallucination vanished.

"I'm Mabel Finch," she said, shoving aside the lamp on the bedside table and setting down the tray. "My husband, Horace, and I own this place. Horace is the one who let you in last night."

She lifted the napkin, exposing a plate covered with crisply fried bacon, scrambled eggs, two delicately browned biscuits, a bowl of gravy and a large mug of coffee. Nick was positive then that she was an angel and he was in heaven. He must have died sometime during the night, probably a heart attack from one of those high-voltage dreams about Analise.

"Th-Thank you," he stammered. "This is great."

Mabel bustled across the room and opened the curtains then leaned back against the dresser, folding her arms across her ample bosom. "Analise wanted you to have a good breakfast. She said you didn't eat anything last night except a handful of cookies."

Analise. He might have known. He drew his fingers over

his stubbled jaw, needing to feel the slight prickle of reality.
"How long have you known Analise?"

"Since about seven this morning. Sit. Eat. You don't
want to be late for church."

"Church?" He plopped onto the edge of the bed.
Damnedest motel he'd ever stayed in. Being served breakfast in his room by the motel owner was nice, but being
sent to church was, he thought, a little pushy. However, it
was a small price to pay for this kind of food.

He unfolded the napkin, picked up the fork and began
to eat.

"Analise told us all about why you're here, looking for
that Abbie Prather person."

Nick broke open a flaky biscuit, poured gravy over it and
crunched another piece of bacon. He wasn't going to let
Analise interfere with this unexpected feast. He *wasn't*.

"Horace and I bought this place ten years ago from the
Claxtons who sold out and moved to Arizona because he
had arthritis and they'd heard the climate was better there.
We're from Wisconsin, so this climate seems better to us.
It's all relative, I guess. Anyway, we don't know Abbie
Prather or June Martin, but if she lives out away from everything and keeps to herself, we might not know her since
we've only been here ten years. I told Analise that the
ministers would be the ones to ask because they know everybody."

Like an embezzler would go to church, Nick thought,
breaking open the second biscuit.

"And sure enough, when Analise called Bob Sampson,
who pastors the Freewill Baptist Church on Grand Avenue,
he told her to come talk to him. Analise said she was sure
you wouldn't mind her borrowing your car and going over
there so we wouldn't have to wake you."

More gravy on that biscuit, Nick ordered himself. *Muffle*

everything this woman is saying with eggs and bacon.
Drown it in coffee.

But it was no use. She had his attention.

Analise had *borrowed* his car? Since he had the only key, that must mean she'd practiced more of her questionable skills and hot-wired it.

"She said to tell you that she'll be back to get you during Sunday school so you can both go to the service at eleven," Mabel continued, then shook her head slowly, the action not disturbing her tight curls. "I don't believe the good Lord will mind if she wears those purple shorts to church, but we're Methodists. I'm not so sure about those Baptists. I offered to loan her one of my dresses, but she wouldn't hear of it."

Purple shorts?

He laid down his fork, drained the cup of coffee and gave up.

Before he was even out of bed, Analise had befriended the motel owners, procured breakfast for him, found a contact who remembered their missing party, stolen his car and gone to church in purple shorts.

And he'd thought he was finished with taking care of, riding herd on and bailing out irresponsible, resourceful females.

Not that his ex-wife, Kay, had ever sent his libido spiraling out of control the way Analise did.

How the heck was he going to keep her out of trouble when he was in major trouble himself?

Analise left the Reverend Robert Sampson's house and headed back to the motel to get Nick so they could go to church and talk to other long-standing members of the congregation who might remember Abbie Prather—a.k.a. June Martin—and Sara.

A vivid picture was emerging of the woman who'd

caused Lucas's family untold agony, and it wasn't a pretty one. She'd been so strict on her daughter that even the Reverend Sampson, a by-the-book clergyman, thought she was cruel rather than dedicated.

The decrepit car Analise had borrowed from Nick inched along the asphalt, so slow she wanted to open the door, put her foot out and push. What a difference from her own car, a small red sporty model with five on the floor and enough power to keep her in regular speeding tickets.

But her car was parked at the Tyler airport while she chugged along in this clunker, fighting her impatience to get back to the motel, back to Nick to share her news with him. Not that she was especially anxious to see him again, or that she felt any need to tell him what she'd accomplished, to prove that she wasn't flaky. It didn't bother her one bit if he thought she was flaky. And after last night, she'd bet her beloved fast red car that he definitely thought she was.

Yesterday had not been one of her diamond days. More like a lump-of-coal day, actually. And Nick had been the crowning lump, a promise of escalating fiascoes to come if she couldn't control her obsessive penchant for flirting with trouble.

Nick was the complete opposite of Lucas. Lucas was safety, security, a friend she could count on. Nick was danger, an invitation to the unknown, to taste the exhilaration of a flight into skies that terrified her even as they tempted her, to prove she could do it.

For most of the night she'd lain awake in the hot little room at the motel, trying to forget the way his accidental touch had made her feel, the way the scent of him had invaded her senses and lingered as surely as if he'd been in that bed with her.

She gripped the steering wheel tightly and ordered herself to stop thinking about that. Not only were those inappropriate feelings for an engaged woman, they were inappropriate feelings for a sane woman. Her bad habit of dancing with disaster usually resulted in a catastrophe rather than success.

She'd left her room early and, to her surprise, found a lead, something she could do to be useful, to take her mind off those hazardous-to-her-health feelings. She'd come up with information that would help them locate Abbie…and rescue Sara.

The familiar sound of a siren intruded on her thoughts.

Automatically her foot hit the brake while her eyes scanned the descending speedometer needle.

Damn! Had she been speeding again? What was the speed limit, anyway? She'd been too caught up in her thoughts to notice.

This decrepit car couldn't possibly be speeding! Maybe the dangling taillight had fallen completely off, or the wire Nick had used to hold up the muffler broke or maybe the car with its three shades of rusty paint and primer violated some law of ugliness.

In her rearview mirror she watched the young officer swagger up to her car.

Swaggering was not a good sign.

She located her driver's license and held it out the window as the man approached. She didn't want him to look too closely inside, to see that she'd hot-wired the car rather than wake Nick to ask for the keys, rather than risk going inside that overheated motel room where he slept, probably in the nude, when she was already overheated.

The policeman accepted her license wordlessly then went back to his car to, she assumed, check for wants and warrants. Good grief! The police in Briar Creek never did that! She could be here all day!

Finally he swaggered back and leaned down to look in,

dark sunglasses hiding his eyes. She leaned toward him so he couldn't see the dangling wires.

"Going a little fast, weren't you, Ms. Brewster?"

And she'd have to go twice as fast to make up for lost time after this. "Only a little," she protested. Why didn't he give her a clue? Tell her what the speed limit was?

"Oh? How fast do you think you were going?"

How did she know what answer she should give when she had no idea what the speed limit was? "Well, I think possibly the speedometer said somewhere around about the vicinity of fifty-eight."

He straightened and began to scribble on his clipboard. "The speed limit through this stretch is forty-five. Big sign a mile back."

Great. An out-of-state ticket to start a brand-new blunder list for today.

"But you see," she improvised, "this car is eleven years old, and since carbon buildup in internal combustion engines results in a gradual slowing of all exposed parts revolving counterclockwise, it's necessary to deduct approximately one mile every year, which means I was only doing forty-seven, and what's a couple of miles between friends?" She gave him her best smile.

The officer stopped writing, lowered his clipboard, raised his sunglasses to his forehead and looked at her. "What?"

"I said—"

"Never mind." He shook his head and replaced his sunglasses. "It's not right, whatever you said. You were doing fifty-nine. Slow down."

"Okay," she agreed. Had her gobbledygook really worked? Was she going to get off without a ticket?

He raised his clipboard again, dashing her hopes with the action. "You didn't signal when you changed lanes, either."

"But there was nobody else on the highway to signal to!"

"You have to obey the law all the time, not just when there's somebody watching. Anyway, I was watching."

She sighed. "All right. From now on I'll signal before changing lanes if it's two o'clock in the morning and I'm in the middle of the Sahara Desert."

"You're not wearing your seat belt."

"It's an old car. The belt's broken."

"I need to see your vehicle registration."

Amazing what a quick downswing her luck had taken in the last few minutes. The way things were going, Nick's contact probably hadn't left them the vehicle registration.

Fumbling in the glove box, she sent up a silent prayer of thanks when she found the document. She gave it to the policeman, leaned her elbow out the window and smiled as innocently as she could.

"This vehicle's registered to Fred Smith of Omaha, Nebraska."

"Yes, it's a borrowed car."

He took a step backward and his hand dropped to his gun. "Borrowed?"

Analise froze. Was she going to be shot for taking Nick's car that wasn't really Nick's car? "Yes, borrowed! You see, my friend...well, he's not really my friend." Oh, dear! She was getting nervous and incoherent. "My detective," she said firmly, pleased with herself for finding the right word, "Nick Claiborne, flew into a small airport and it was late and his friend...well, I don't know if it was his friend or just an acquaintance...anyway, he left him this car and I borrowed it this morning because I had to go to church and find out about Abbie Prather who's now June Martin and—"

"Turn off your engine and step out of the vehicle."

Turn off the engine? Dive under the dash and untwist the wires? Not a good idea.

Leaving the car running, she opened the door and slid out. "If you'll just call Nick at the…oh, dear, I can't remember the name of the motel, but it's down the highway a couple of miles, which is why I was heading that way except you can't call him because there aren't any phones in the rooms but Mabel has a phone…"

Nick stood on the sidewalk in front of his room in the still-cool, bright Sunday morning. From the outside, the old motel with its peeling paint and missing room numbers had a quaint charm. In other circumstances, he'd have considered the day to be perfect, a good omen. But as he waited for Analise to show up in his borrowed car that she'd so cavalierly reborrowed, he had a bad feeling.

A large, older-model black car pulled up. His gaze flicked over the automobile and returned to searching the highway for any signs of the rust-colored—or covered—vehicle Analise had absconded with.

Mabel's head popped out the window of the passenger side of the black car. "Analise just called. She needs you to get her out of jail."

As Nick rode with the Finches to the Prairieview police station, he marveled that these people whom Analise hadn't known twenty-four hours ago leaped to her defense.

"It's Frank Marshall's youngest boy," Mabel explained. "He's been watching too many cop shows on television. Nothing ever happens in Prairieview, so he goes around looking for trouble. Gave Mildred Adams a ticket for parking too close to a fire hydrant. Took a tape measure and got her at four inches too close. Imagine, taking Analise in just because the car wasn't registered in her name."

Apparently Analise hadn't mentioned in her phone call

to Mabel Finch that she'd hot-wired his car. That undoubtedly contributed to the arresting officer's suspicions.

Ten minutes later they were in the middle of the Sunday-silent town. Mannequins in the department store window stood motionless, gazing from painted eyes at the empty sofas and chairs on display in the furniture store across the street. The movie theater marquee had a couple of letters missing. Even the drugstore was deserted. Anyone needing an antacid or deodorant would, Nick presumed, have to wait until Monday.

Horace pulled up next to Nick's rented car, in front of the small, weathered-rock building designated as the Prairieview Police Station by the words carved above the door.

Both Horace and Mabel started to get out, but Nick stopped them. "You all go on to church. I don't want you to be late. I'll take care of Analise."

"Well, okay," Horace agreed reluctantly. "But if you run into any trouble, you call us at the Methodist church and we'll come talk to Frank's boy."

Nick thanked them, exited the car, walked up to the building and grasped the tarnished brass handle to yank open the front door. He'd take care of Analise all right. After he got her out of jail, he'd wring her slender neck.

The door proved to be heavier than he'd thought and reluctant to move, so his dramatic gesture was lost. Instead, it creaked slowly open.

Analise and a young man in a blue uniform looked up as he entered. The man sat behind a desk with Analise in a chair in front. In the first instant, his mind registered that she was indeed wearing purple shorts with a scoop-necked, sleeveless blouse with bright flowers of purple, black, yellow and a green the same color as her eyes. She'd wrapped a long purple tie around the neck he was getting ready to wring, and the ends floated down her back. She sat with one long leg crossed over the other, a purple sandal adorning her slim foot. She was as bright and tempting and dangerous as the neon lights of Las Vegas.

In the second instant, he noted that she held five cards in her hand and had a pile of pennies in front of her.

Horror washed over him as he recalled the dubious skills her former boyfriend had taught her. She was playing poker with the cop who'd arrested her and dealing off the bottom of the deck, judging by the size of her pile of pennies as compared to the officer's pile.

She gave him her dazzling smile just as he charged across the room and snatched the cards out of her fingers, sending the rest of the deck and her ill-gotten pennies flying. It also sent him tumbling into her lap.

How was it possible, in a moment of crisis, that he still noticed she smelled like honeysuckle on a warm summer evening and her skin was as soft and velvety as the petals of a magnolia blossom?

He pushed himself up, endeavoring to get his face out of her midriff and his hands off her thighs, even though his body would have loved to stay right there.

As he struggled to his feet, his gaze met her startled green eyes. *Startled, but not horrified,* some alien creature in the back of his brain exulted. Startled and maybe just a little bit…excited?

"Hold it right there, mister!"

Nick whirled around to see the officer standing with his weapon drawn.

Great. He was going to end up in jail with Analise, both of them growing old and fat together, eating fried eggs and bologna for breakfast every morning. And the way things were going, she'd be in a cell close enough for him to hear her talk all day long but not close enough to touch.

"It's okay, Joe," Analise reassured the officer. "This is Nick Claiborne, the man whose car I borrowed. Tell him I didn't steal it, Nick."

Joe reholstered his gun but didn't relax. "Car's not registered to Nick Claiborne."

"I *told* you—" Analise began impatiently, but Joe cut her off.

"You got any proof you rented it from Fred Smith?" He sneered at Nick.

"Have you got any proof I didn't?" Nick withdrew his wallet, opened it to his private investigator's license and slammed it onto the desk. "I'm working on a case. Ms. Brewster is my client. I rented the car, and she took it to use this morning."

"With your permission?"

Nick gritted his teeth but made himself lie. "Yes."

"Then how come she had to hot-wire it?"

There was a limit to how big a lie he could tell. He avoided the question instead. "What are the charges against Ms. Brewster?"

Joe stood straighter. "Speeding, failure to signal before changing lanes, failure to wear a seat belt and possibly driving a stolen vehicle."

"Has the car been reported stolen?"

Joe slumped back into his chair. "No," he admitted grudgingly.

"Then write her tickets for the rest and let her go."

Joe waved one hand negligibly. "Aw, we'll just forget about the tickets. Analise explained why she was speeding, there wasn't anybody around to signal to anyway and the seat belt was broken."

"Thanks, Joe!" Analise beamed at the officer then bent and started retrieving her pennies.

Nick grabbed her arm and dragged her from the station.

"What on earth is the matter with you?" she demanded, jerking away from his grasp as soon as they were outside.

"Bad enough you were cheating at cards with a police

officer, I wasn't about to let you take your winnings with you."

She fisted her hands on her curved, purple-silk-clad hips. "I wasn't cheating! How could you possibly think I would cheat?"

"You're the one who told me your friend taught you to deal off the bottom of the deck!"

"I assume you know how to shoot a gun, too, but you don't go around doing it for fun!"

Nick threw his arms into the air. "I learned how to shoot a gun when I went through the police academy. The purpose was to save my life. I haven't shot one since I left the force. Do you want to explain to me how that relates to cheating at cards?"

"I...was...not...cheating!" She bent forward at the waist and ground out each word from between clenched teeth. "And you never know when being able to deal from the bottom of the deck could save your life."

"How?"

"Well..." Her voice trailed off and she moved around him toward the car, then stopped and faced him again. "You never know until the situation arises. It's always best to be prepared."

He unlocked the car door and opened it. "Get in."

"Not until you apologize for accusing me of cheating."

"If you weren't cheating, how did you win all those pennies?"

She shrugged, the movement shifting the brightly colored fabric that covered her rounded breasts in a tantalizing manner. "Beginner's luck."

"Beginner's luck? What about the story of your boyfriend teaching you to play poker?"

"Well, sure, he taught me, but we never really played, just practiced. When I saw a deck of cards on the desk in there, I figured I might as well give it a shot. What did I have to lose? If you hadn't charged in like some maniac, I was getting ready to offer him double or nothing to drop the charges against me. I had a royal flush. Joe dealt me the ace, queen, jack and ten of hearts and then I drew the king.''

With a final glare, she turned and slid into the car then closed the door.

Now, how the hell had she managed to make him feel guilty, when she'd stolen his car, gotten herself thrown in jail and he'd rescued her? At least Kay had been grateful when he'd gotten her out of her scrapes.

He strode around to the driver's side, resisting an impulse to smack the hood as he passed. The car might fall completely apart.

Damn it, she'd hired him to do a job, to vindicate her fiancé's father and find the guilty party. Nothing in that job description required him to look out for her when she got herself in a mess. He solved other people's problems from a safe distance. He didn't get involved, not with the problem or the client. That's what he liked about this job. No emotions. No ups, no downs, no worries, no losses.

He got in the car and slammed the door…hard. The vehicle quivered and rattled but remained in one piece.

"I don't care what it takes," he said, "even if it costs me a day's investigation, even if you decide to fire me, you are, as of this minute, on your way back to Texas."

Distress clouded Analise's features. "I can't do that. Bob—Reverend Sampson—told me that June Martin— that's the name he knew her by—that her daughter, Sara, not only had red hair like me but also green eyes and she even spelled her name the way I spelled my doll's name when I was a little girl. With no 'h' on the end." She lifted both hands as if to forestall his protest. "I know, I know. Could be coincidences, but I believe I have a connection with Sara. I believe fate brought me here so I could intervene in her life and help her get over the cruel things her mother did to her. I have to be there when you find her. It's my destiny. I have wonderful parents, a stable home life, terrific friends, all the material things I could possibly want—I've always had life handed to me on a silver platter and now it's my turn to pass along some of the good stuff."

There was no mistaking the sincerity, the concern, in her voice and in her eyes. At the same time as a part of Nick raged in protest, another part melted at her misplaced desire to help someone less fortunate.

Her long, golden legs, generous lips and rounded breasts that moved those improbable flowers on her blouse up and down and all around with every breath undoubtedly had something to do with his meltdown, but he couldn't think about that.

If they did make it to church, he'd most certainly pray that they found June and Sara Martin before nightfall and Analise would be out of his life forever.

"Bob told me that June and Sara moved away right after Sara started school," Analise informed him, as if her sole purpose in life was to complicate his.

The fact that some rebellious, not-very-bright part of him gave a tiny, embarrassed cheer at the thought of Analise not disappearing from his life forever only proved how desperately he needed to get away from her.

Chapter Three

Analise had always considered herself fairly adept at reading people's expressions, but Nick's facial contortions had her totally confused. He was bound to be a little upset at having to retrieve her from jail, and she hadn't expected him to be thrilled at the news that their quarry had left Nebraska. However, his eyes alternately brightened and darkened as they darted from her head to her feet and back again. His lips compressed tightly even as the corner seemed to be trying to turn up in some sort of smile or grimace.

Finally he looked away and put the key in the ignition. "Can I drive this thing now or do you need to hot-wire it first?"

"I put everything back just the way it was." She wanted to tell him that she wasn't real thrilled at the idea of spending more time with him, either...with somebody who thought she was the type who would cheat at cards. But she didn't think that would be a wise idea right now.

Besides, it wasn't entirely true. Some part of her deep

inside, some self-destructive part of her, was just the tiniest bit thrilled at the idea of spending more time with him. Actually, it was more than a tiny bit thrilled.

Whatever odd thoughts he'd been having as his gaze had raked her from head to foot, one element was always there...the heat. He'd sent her adrenaline surging, poured gasoline on those smoldering lumps of coal she thought she'd doused until he fell into her lap in the police station. Hardly a sensuous action, yet somehow it had been. She didn't want to even think about the feel of his face buried against her stomach, his hand on her thigh.

Didn't want to think about it but couldn't seem to stop.

"Well," Nick said, his curt tone slicing into her thoughts, "you've certainly had a busy morning. So where are we off to now? Church? Back to hear more from the Reverend Sampson?"

"No. Now we need to go to the Presbyterian church."

"Ah, a conversion!"

"There's no call for sarcasm. It's where Sara's grade-school principal goes. Sampson thinks he'd probably remember where they moved to."

Nick grunted and mumbled something.

"What?"

"I said, that's a good lead. Any idea where the Presbyterian church is located?"

"Yes, I have quite specific directions."

As Nick drove, Analise kept her gaze turned away from his chiseled profile, his tousled hair, his hands that had touched her body. Those thoughts were not only dangerous but also disloyal to Lucas. Instead, she focused out the car window, watching the older houses with their neatly tended lawns roll past. Prairieview had the same sleepy small-town atmosphere as Briar Creek. The only real difference was the terrain, the flat Nebraska prairie instead of lushly green, gently rolling hills. But it had the same quiet, reverent Sunday-morning air of home, and she had the same embarrassed, inept feeling she ended up with so often at home.

Amazing. She'd started out the day so good, doing everything right, then managed to get herself thrown into jail and had to ask Nick to rescue her. And Nick thought she was cheating at cards. That bothered her as much as anything. For as long as she could remember, she'd been a little blunder-prone, but nobody had ever accused her of being dishonest.

Until today.

Until Nick.

It shouldn't matter what Nick thought of her, but it did. And that bothered her. Trying to prove herself to somebody like Nick could only result in major problems. She'd seen proof of that already this morning.

Oh, brother! She'd just admitted to herself that she wanted to prove herself to Nick, to impress him, to fly into the face of the storm and beat back the wind. Fat chance.

"All right," Nick said, interrupting her gloomy contemplation. "Tell me in detail about your conversation with the Reverend Sampson."

She looked over at him. His square jaw was set resolutely, but at least he wanted to discuss the good part of the morning. "Bob Sampson remembered June Martin very clearly. She came to his church every week and she worked at the bank."

"That's interesting. Did any money disappear along with her when she left town?"

"I asked him that and he said no. Either she didn't want to push her luck or she got better at hiding her crimes. He said she was kind of a religious fanatic. She and her daughter went to every service, but they never made friends, never participated in social activities. He said Sara was a very quiet, subdued little girl, that June ruled her with an iron hand and Sara seemed scared of her mother."

"That's too bad."

He sounded disconnected, detached, as though they were talking about the mechanical breakdown of a car or something. "It certainly is too bad! Where were the authorities? Why didn't somebody help Sara? Why didn't Sampson do something about it? He's supposed to help people!"

"Hey, don't get mad at me. I'm agreeing with you. But you've got to be realistic here. That was a long time ago, a small town, and what could the authorities do anyway? Did she beat Sara? Did she hurt her physically?"

"She spanked her. Sampson saw her do that in church. And she probably did worse in private. How else could she subdue her so drastically? Remember you said when she was in Wyoming that she'd been, and I quote, *a pistol*. June Martin had to do something drastic to break her spirit like that."

He stared straight ahead through the windshield, his profile calm and unperturbed though his jaw was still set solidly, with one muscle twitching slightly as if maintaining that calm was an effort. "I'm sure you're right, but that was a lot of years ago. Sara's grown now, probably has a good job, a husband, maybe a couple of kids. Whatever happened to her as a child is over and done with. We'll find June Martin and she'll go to jail for embezzlement and you're going to have to accept that as her punishment for whatever she did wrong in raising her daughter."

"I can't believe you're so uncaring about this whole thing!"

Nick pulled into the Presbyterian church's parking lot and turned to Analise. "I can't believe you're getting so upset about somebody you don't even know."

For a long moment Analise stared into the distant, unreadable blue of Nick's gaze and questioned exactly why she was so obsessed with Sara's happiness. Obviously it only added to her instability in Nick's eyes. On the other hand, she couldn't accept his total lack of concern.

"I can't explain it, but Sara doesn't feel like a stranger. It's like there's some sort of a link between her and me. I felt it last night when you first told me about her. Then today when Sampson was talking about her, it was almost like I could feel her sadness and loneliness. Like I was destined to find that little girl who has the same color hair and eyes that I do, find her and rescue her from the awful woman who caused so many problems for so many people."

Nick lifted one eyebrow skeptically.

"Fine," she said, turning away and reaching for the door handle. "I don't care whether or not you believe me. I don't care whether or not you keep working for me. I'll do it without you."

"Analise—" He laid a restraining hand on her shoulder, and those tingles started again, her already warm skin warming in a different way, setting those lumps of coal to blazing again.

She held her breath, paralyzed, unable or unwilling to move. His hand slid slowly down her arm, lighting miniature forest fires everywhere it touched, and he made a sound that was somewhere between a sigh and a moan. Or maybe the sound came from her own throat. Or maybe she only imagined it.

This wasn't good at all. Okay, it felt good, real good, but she didn't need some man other than her fiancé making her feel things her fiancé didn't. Not that she wanted to feel those things from her fiancé, that out-of-control, wildly exciting ride on the Adrenaline River straight over Disaster Falls.

She definitely didn't need this, didn't want or need to be attracted to a man who was the embodiment of chaos, guaranteed to create more problems in her life.

Nick took his hand away, and she opened the car door and darted out. He caught up to her as they reached the church steps.

"Analise, I didn't mean to imply that I don't believe you. I just have a hard time understanding. I helped raise four little sisters and I was married for four months, so I know what it means to be compelled to take care of someone and worry about them. But—a stranger?"

She stopped and turned back to him. "I've always had everything. It's been great, but I've often wondered why I should be so lucky. I didn't do anything to deserve any of it. And Sara didn't do anything to deserve so much bad. It's not fair that I had so much and she had so little. Maybe this is my chance to make things more equal."

He stared at her for a long moment, his gaze unreadable and veiled. Finally he shrugged. "Whatever. It's your case." He looked down at her bare legs. "But are you sure you want to go to church in that getup?"

She lifted her chin defiantly. "Last I heard, God was more concerned with the inside than the outside. Anyway, I don't have anything else. This bag will only hold so much."

Nick scowled. "Why didn't you bring a regular suitcase?"

"If my parents had seen me packing a suitcase, they'd have stopped me from coming. If anybody in that town had seen me with a suitcase, they'd have told my parents, who'd have stopped me from coming."

Nick's gaze moved slowly over her body, heating her blood as if he'd physically touched her, then returning to her face. "You're a grown woman. Isn't that a little extreme, having the whole town tattling on you?"

"I've always thought so. I told you, my parents are really into being overprotective. I'm twenty-seven years old, but you'd think I was still seven the way they treat me. They don't think I have sense enough to cross the street by myself even though there's hardly any traffic in Briar Creek, which reminds me, I haven't called them since I got to the airport in Wyoming yesterday and they'll be worried. I need to find a phone.''

"Do your parents have reason to worry about you?''

She glared at him, unable to answer the question since she had no intention of admitting they did, but she couldn't very well lie while standing on the front steps of a church.

Fortunately the door opened, the congregation surged out between them and she didn't have to answer Nick's insulting question.

"Excuse me,'' she said to a well-dressed, well-powdered elderly lady, "I'm looking for Winston Turnbull. Is he here today? Could you point him out to me?''

The woman looked around. "I don't see him right now, but he's here. You can't miss that off-key voice during the hymns. He'll be out shortly, I'm sure. Looks like a bald-headed grasshopper wearing a blue suit.''

"Thank you.''

She pushed through the stream of people to where Nick stood, still scowling, his arms folded across his chest. "Sara's principal is here—'' she began, but he cut her off.

"I heard. Do you want me to do this or would you rather take over and I'll go home?''

"I was trying to help.''

He plowed one hand through his hair and blew out a long breath. "I know. But I'd just as soon you didn't help. Okay? If you want me to handle this, I will. If you don't, I'll turn it over to you and head back home.''

A few minutes ago she'd threatened to do it herself, but she was very well aware that was all talk. On her own, she'd not only fail to find June and Sara, she'd probably get lost herself. "I don't want you to go home. This is very important to me, especially now that we know about Sara. I'd have a hard time finding them on my own.''

Nick's gaze shifted to over her shoulder. "I think that may be Principal Turnbull."

He moved toward a man who certainly fit the description given her by the woman she'd questioned.

Analise followed closely behind. Nick might think he didn't need her help but he could be wrong.

Nick guided the rattletrap car into the crowded parking lot of Sophie's Diner. Despite his austere appearance, Winston Turnbull had proven friendly and willing to talk to them, provided they'd accompany him to lunch. "Since my wife, Lucy, died seven years ago," he'd said, "I'm always at Sophie's by 12:10. She'll have a platter of fried chicken waiting for me, and my stomach's waiting for it. Church is a hungry business. They should have recess and refreshments, the way we do at school."

Nick maneuvered the car into a parking space and killed the engine. Maybe for good.

"This is so exciting," Analise said. "Everybody we talk to adds a little piece to the puzzle of Sara and June."

Nick noted that Analise's obsession had changed from *Abbie Prather/June Martin* to *Sara and June,* with Sara's name coming first. This whole situation was making him very uncomfortable, and not only because he couldn't keep his hormones under control around Analise or even because he wasn't sure what catastrophe she might create next.

Her presence was making this case a personal event, turning all the names that should be faceless into real people. That wasn't safe. If he hadn't learned that lesson adequately before he joined the police force in Tyler ten years ago, that experience had certainly reinforced it.

For the past two years as a private investigator, he'd survived by maintaining an emotional distance from the people and situations. Analise was making that very difficult now, especially since he had to contend not only with her very real, very personal person, but now she was turning Sara Martin into a flesh-and-blood, breathing, feeling, real person.

"I hope Turnbull adds the missing piece and we can find them soon," he said. Before he started worrying about Analise and Sara and whether he could fix everything for them.

"Me, too." She opened her car door and slid out.

Nick followed suit, hurrying to catch up with her as she dashed toward Winston. Analise did everything in fast forward.

As they entered the small, crowded restaurant, Nick was concerned at first that they wouldn't find a table, but Winston led them straight to an empty booth. "It's always reserved for me," he said, sliding into one side and motioning them to the other.

Analise slid in first and Nick followed her, sitting on an uneven surface that tilted him toward the center, plop up against Analise.

"Excuse me," he muttered, pushing himself away from her.

Apparently, Winston's usual luncheon companion was someone of large proportions who left a depression exactly in the middle of the seat.

"What'll you folks have?" the waitress asked.

Nick scrambled for the plastic-covered menu as he fought to maintain his position, perched half in and half out of the valley between Analise and him.

"Fried chicken for me." Analise sounded perky and enthusiastic in spite of what were, to her, probably unfamiliar surroundings, not exactly the exclusive restaurants she doubtlessly frequented at home. "I love fried chicken. And a cola. A big one, please." Although he shouldn't be surprised. She'd weathered the local motel and the local jail. Why would the local diner bother her?

"I'll have the chicken, too," he said. No way could he concentrate on the menu and maintain his precarious position at the same time. "And iced tea."

"Do you remember Sara Martin?" she asked Winston as soon as the waitress left, and Nick cringed at the hopeful eagerness in her voice. She was doing it again, taking this case away from him, away from being a business deal, and turning it into something personal.

"If you can give us any information about Sara Martin or her mother, we'd very much appreciate it," he said, trying to deflect the emotion, retrieve the business aspect.

Winston Turnbull draped a long arm over the back of the seat. "I've been the principal of our elementary school for forty years next fall. During that time I've seen a lot of children come and go. Many of them I've forgotten, but that little girl, I remember even though she only attended through the first grade."

The waitress returned to set glasses of iced tea in front of Nick and Winston, and a large glass of cola in front of Analise. Winston stirred three packets of sugar into his tea.

"So you do remember Sara," Nick encouraged.

"Oh, yes. She was a distinctive little girl with those big green eyes and that red hair." He took a sip of tea, set his glass down and studied Analise carefully, his high forehead wrinkling halfway across his bald skull. "What's your reason for wanting to find these people?"

"My fiancé's father—" Analise began, but Nick cut off the involved explanation he knew was coming up.

"It's a long story. They're from my client's hometown and connected to her fiancé."

Winston nodded slowly. "Are you Sara?" he asked abruptly.

Nick lost his balance and slid into the gully, bumping

against Analise's soft, fragrant body. The whole world went a little fuzzy as all his senses centered on the parts of him that touched her, as if nothing else mattered, nothing else was real.

He heard her sharp intake of breath but didn't dare look at her. If he did, if she wasn't outraged and repulsed, if he saw even a spark of the same desire he felt, the way he'd seen that spark when he'd tumbled into her lap at the police station, he might never be able to climb out of this hole in the middle of the bench in Sophie's Diner. He might stay here forever, savoring the tantalizing sensations that resulted from touching her, the way his blood danced a little jig on its way to pool in the nether regions of his body.

He struggled out and back to his perch. How the hell was he going to eat fried chicken while performing this balancing act?

"You okay?" Winston asked.

"Yeah, sure, I'm fine."

"You look a little flushed and you're perspiring even though Sophie's got the air on high."

Maybe the problem last night in the motel room hadn't been with the air-conditioning at all, but merely the way Analise had of raising his temperature…by making him crazy with her antics and with her touch.

"In answer to your question, no, I'm not Sara," Analise said, and he thought she sounded slightly breathless, an almost undetectable sign that she was as flustered as he by their collision.

"Forgive my impertinent question, but you bear a strong resemblance to her. I know people change over the years, but you've got the same color hair and eyes. I thought perhaps you'd been adopted out and were trying to find your real mother, the way they do on that television show."

"No, I wasn't adopted out," Analise said softly. "I was born and grew up in Briar Creek, Texas. That's where June

Martin's from, and I really need to find her and her daughter. Maybe there's something in the school records..."

Winston trailed a long finger down his glass of tea, his gaze on the path he was making through the condensation. "I can't help you."

Analise heaved a deep sigh of dismay.

"I'm sorry," Winston said, looking up at her. His expression and his voice said he meant it. There was room for negotiation here. "I wish I could, but school records are private, and I can't give them out to just anybody."

"But I'm not just anybody," Analise pleaded.

Winston smiled gently. "I know. I really am sorry, but rules are rules."

The food arrived on large, thick platters, each holding assorted pieces of crispy fried chicken, mashed potatoes and gravy, green beans with bacon pieces. To this feast the waitress added a basket of dinner rolls, obviously homemade.

Nick dived in with a vengeance. After the huge breakfast, he wasn't particularly hungry, but he needed to divert his attention from Analise sitting so close, from the knowledge that if he let himself relax for a second, he'd slide against her and this time he might not make it out of that gulf.

Analise's arm brushed his as she reached for her drink. He pressed his arm more tightly to his side in spite of its efforts to take off on its own and connect with hers again.

"Tell me what she was like," Analise requested of Winston. Nick turned toward her, trying to catch her eye, to signal to her that she should let it go for a while. If they had any chance of getting this man to divulge any information, they needed to catch him off guard.

But she was entirely focused on her goal and refused to look his way.

Winston laid down his half-eaten drumstick, blotted his mouth with his napkin and looked into the distance as if recalling the past when he'd known the little red-haired girl. "She was kind of shy but bright and funny when you could get her to relax. She always made straight A's and was never a discipline problem."

"Was she happy?"

Leave it to Analise to go straight to the heart.

Winston shrugged. "It's hard to say." He picked up his chicken then laid it down again and frowned. "I don't think she was. She didn't smile much, didn't have many friends. That mother of hers was awfully strict. She brought her to school every morning and picked her up after."

"No sign of a father?"

"None."

Analise was silent for a few moments, but he should have known it was too good to last.

"Do you have kids?" At least she'd changed the subject.

"Yes, I have two children, a girl and a boy, and three grandchildren."

"That's nice." Her voice held a wistful tone. "I'm an only child. I always wanted a brother or sister. I think it's really bizarre that Sara and I look so much alike and we came from the same town, like maybe there's a psychic connection."

Oh, great! She was going to tell this man her life history, including this fancied link to Sara Martin.

He nudged her foot with his, and she pulled her foot away.

Did she think he was flirting with her? He could feel the perspiration gathering again, but he ignored it. If he wiped the dampness away, that would be admitting he was nervous.

Analise talked in her animated fashion, waved her hands, laughed, and even as Nick's nerves stood on edge, something in her enthusiasm, her ardor, her passion beckoned to him, teasing those nerves. He thought of what she'd said about daring to do that which frightened a person the most, and he understood.

Analise's passion scared him. Emotions scared him. At the same time, he wanted to dive in, wallow in her exuberance, suck it all up in what he knew would be a lethal dose.

His calm, uneventful life with his widower dad had been disrupted at age ten when his father had married a woman with two little girls, six and three. His stepmother had shortly thereafter produced twins for a total of four chattering females, four sisters he'd helped care for and grown to love beyond reason. Four girls who'd taken over and totally changed his life. Six months after the twins, Paula and Peggy, left for college, he'd married Kay...just before she got evicted from her apartment for nonpayment of rent. To his intense relief, she'd left four months later, riding away on the back of a motorcycle with a man she met in her pottery class.

And he was finished with caretaking. He had his own life now, and it was a good one. The last thing he needed was another chattering woman full of passion and wayward emotions who needed to be taken care of. Another woman who'd disrupt his world then walk away without a backward glance.

She was already ruining his interview technique. Now Winston was telling her about his deceased wife and his grandkids' grades in school and positions on the local baseball teams.

Suddenly Winston folded his napkin and laid it beside his empty plate. For a thin man, he sure had put away that lunch. Nick still had most of his left. Analise had eaten every bite on her plate. No surprise there. Creating chaos took a lot of calories.

Winston smiled at Analise. "Why don't you two ride

over to the school with me, and perhaps I could find something in the old records to help you after all?''

The shock released Nick's tenuous hold on his seat, and he slid into Analise again. To his chagrin and utter delight, she threw her arms around him. ''Isn't that wonderful, Nick? Thank you, Winston!''

Wonderful.

Yes, it was wonderful, feeling her body pressed against his like that. Wonderful. Exciting. Stimulating. Exhilarating. Dangerous. Seductive.

He couldn't stop himself from looking directly into her eyes.

And what he saw there scared him even more.

He had no doubt she'd thrown her arms around him in enthusiastic innocence, but the way her eyes darkened, the green changing from oak leaf to magnolia leaf, the way her lush lips parted slightly, told him she felt the sparks that zipped between them.

The need to kiss her grew as strong as the need to breathe. More than he wanted to fly, more than he'd wanted the breakfast Mabel had brought this morning, he wanted to kiss Analise Brewster.

One taste, he told himself. One taste of those luscious lips would surely satisfy his craving.

Yeah, like one drink satisfied an alcoholic's craving.

If they hadn't been in a public restaurant, he wouldn't have been able to resist.

One of them had to get on the road back to Texas...fast. This town wasn't big enough for the two of them. Heck, New York City wouldn't be big enough for the two of them.

Chapter Four

The elementary school was small and old and brought back so many memories of her own school days, Analise hesitated at the door of the principal's office. She'd gone through a similar door more than a couple of times, and not, on those occasions, to get information from a considerate principal like Winston.

Winston unlocked it and waved her into the outer office.

The large wooden desk held a computer instead of a typewriter, but was, in other aspects, very similar to the one in Briar Creek where she'd spent many tense hours. The plastic chairs where incorrigible students waited to be sentenced could have been the same ones she'd fidgeted in. Even the faintly musty, *bookish* smell was the same.

"Have a seat," Winston instructed, and disappeared into a storeroom.

She considered one of the *waiting* chairs, but decided to stand instead. Nick perched on the edge of the secretary's desk, folded his arms across his chest and stared into space.

Alone with Nick in the principal's office...either element

was enough to shoot her nervous quotient right through the acoustical ceiling tiles. Put those two elements together, and the roof was in danger.

In the restaurant, she'd been ready to order a piece of pie, when Winston suggested they come over here and thereby rescued her. Not that she was hungry after that huge lunch. Just that she needed to keep eating, to give herself something to do besides think about sliding into that canyon in the middle of the seat and bumping smack into Nick's body. She was amazed nobody but her had noticed the fireworks going off every time that happened. Maybe they were all inside her, but it sure felt as though they detonated everywhere his body touched hers.

And then she'd hugged him!

Okay, so she was a hugger. It was pure reflex. She hugged everybody. But from now on she was going to have to exclude Nick from her definition of *everybody*. There was something dangerous and frightening and altogether thrilling in the way it felt to hug Nick. Not even in the same category as the warm, safe way it felt to hug Lucas.

She dared to look at Nick again. He hadn't moved.

"This is so exciting," she said exuberantly. "Getting a lead to Sara's whereabouts," she clarified in case he was able to read her mind and see her wayward thoughts.

He turned his blue-steel gaze on her, a gaze that made her pretty sure he could read her mind. "Somehow I don't find waiting in the principal's office very exciting."

"Don't tell me you got into trouble in school, too?" That was a smooth move. She'd just admitted to him that she'd been in trouble in school. Added to the morning's events, it wasn't likely to enhance his confidence in her. Not that it mattered. "What did you do wrong?" Maybe she could divert the discussion to his misdemeanors.

For a long moment she didn't think he was going to

answer her. "From the fifth grade on, it was mostly fights," he finally said.

That was no surprise, considering how angry he always seemed to be. "What happened? Did you accuse the other kids of cheating?" She folded her own arms as if in imitation of him, but really to bolster herself against that unblinking gaze.

He blinked then, a couple of times and returned his stare to the wall above her head. "Most of the fights were because of my sisters."

"You were defending your sisters? Oh, I think that's sweet!" And it gave him a new dimension, made him even more attractive, like a bomb wrapped in silver paper with a big red bow on top.

He looked at her, one eyebrow lifted. "Sweet?" He shook his head. "I had four sisters, and the youngest—twins—were just starting school when I was a senior. I always had at least one tagging along and usually they came in pairs, wanting to play baseball, go fishing, go with me on dates. And there'd always be some bully who'd say something rude about one of them, so I'd have to shove his words down his throat. Getting my eyes blackened on a regular basis was not sweet."

"So do I take this to mean you let them play baseball, fish, go on your dates? I hope you never got into fights with your dates." She grinned.

He ducked his head and rubbed the back of his neck. When he lifted his head again, he wasn't actually smiling, but his lips had relaxed into something that kind of resembled a smile if you looked at it just the right way. "No, I didn't get into fights with my dates. But if some girl had a problem with my kid sisters, I just didn't go out with her again. Played hell with my social life."

"You must have really loved your sisters. I don't care what you say, that's sweet."

His steely gaze softened, though his voice was gruff when he replied. "Of course I loved my sisters. That doesn't mean they didn't drive me crazy. They did. They're all out on their own now, and I'm enjoying every minute of the peace and solitude. At least I was."

Until you came along. He didn't say the words, but Analise heard them anyway. Until she came tagging along, getting into trouble, causing problems for him to fix.

Like two streams that merged, one icy and one boiling, anger mingled with hurt that rippled through her at the implied criticism...anger at herself. What on earth was the matter with her that she'd be attracted to someone who didn't even like her? Had there been a rebellion with her hormones usurping power and relegating her brain to some dark prison cell? Where was her loyalty to her fiancé? She gave herself a mental kick.

"Here we go," Winston said, and she turned to see him emerging from the storeroom, brushing dust from his Sunday-best blue suit with one hand while brandishing a file in the other. He took a seat behind the desk and opened the folder. "It would appear they moved to Wanitka, Minnesota. I have a letter from the school requesting we transfer Sara's records."

Nick leaned forward, peering at the papers. "I don't suppose you've got a birth certificate in there."

Winston looked up and closed the file. "Yes," he said, his tone bordering between protective primness and uncertainty, "but all this information is confidential."

"Please?" Analise entreated. "If we knew who Sara's father was, it might help us find her." As well as prove to Nick that Lucas's father was not Sara's father.

Winston's gaze flickered over her, and he smiled. "Are you sure you're not Sara? You certainly bring back memories of that little girl. That's the same intense look she used to get when she didn't understand something but was determined to learn it.'' He reopened the folder and flipped through the contents. "I've thought about her a lot. Worried about her, actually. She had so much potential, but I've wondered many times over the years if she was ever able to utilize it. That mother of hers was something else." He shook his head and rose. "If you'll excuse me, I need to check on something in my office. I'll be back in five minutes."

He went through the connecting door and closed it, leaving the file open on his desk.

Analise leaned over it at the same time as Nick. Her head collided with his as his scents of denim, soap and masculinity collided with her senses. "Sorry," she mumbled, backing away and not daring to look at him, knowing that penetrating gaze would see right through to her inexplicable, shameful feelings.

From the corner of her eye she saw that he, too, had pulled back. She leaned forward again.

And bumped into him again.

Nervous giggles spilled from her lips and tumbled into the silence of the room. "We gotta quit meeting like this," she said, then laughed even more at the inanity of her comment.

Nick didn't laugh. The corners of his mouth twitched, but she couldn't tell if he was fighting a smile or a frown, and he had that strange expression again.

He turned abruptly from her and picked up the photocopy of a birth certificate from the file. "The man's only giving us five minutes to snoop. Let's not waste it."

For no good reason, that struck Analise as funny, too, but she squelched her giggles, went around the desk and checked through the rest of the papers in the thin folder.

"Listen to this. It's Sara's evaluation, written by Winston. *Sara Martin is bright and eager to learn, but extremely shy and unsure of herself. She does not mingle well with other children at recess. Single parent, June Martin, unwilling to meet with me to discuss any problems. She brings the child to school and picks her up after class even if other children are participating in after-school activities. Sara seems to fear her mother. I suspect problems at home, perhaps emotional if not physical abuse.* Oh, Nick! We have to find her soon!''

Nick was writing in a small spiral-bound notebook which he returned to his shirt pocket. He shook his head and Analise lifted her chin. ''I know, I know. She's probably married and has children now. I don't care. That just means we've already wasted far too much time.''

''Very well, I'm finished in here,'' Winston said loudly from his inner office.

Analise and Nick fumbled to return the papers to the file, and even under those stressful conditions, Analise was appalled to find that she noticed the feel of his hands brushing against hers, the rough texture of the balls of his fingers, the slight prickle of hair on his knuckles, the unyielding sinews and, most of all, those blasted fireworks again, exploding along every nerve ending in her fingers.

When she heard the door behind them open, Analise darted over to give Winston an impulsive hug. ''Thank you,'' she said. ''Not just for helping us but for caring about Sara.''

He blushed and Nick came around to shake his hand.

''Good luck to both of you. I hope you find Sara and that she *is* married and happy with a couple of red-haired children.''

''Me, too.'' But Analise had an uneasy feeling.

Winston remained in his office while Analise followed Nick out of the building, striding as fast as she could to keep up with him.

''Who's Sara's father?'' she demanded as soon as they were outside in the parking lot.

"I don't know." Nick opened the car door for her to get in.

"You mean June didn't name anybody on the birth certificate?"

"She named someone." He closed the passenger door behind her and went around to the driver's side.

"For goodness's sake, tell me!" she urged as soon as he got in.

As if to deliberately annoy her, Nick started the car, checked the mirrors, then clenched both hands on the steering wheel before he answered. "Albert Martin."

"See, I told you Wayne Daniels wasn't her father!"

He scowled. "I don't think Albert Martin is, either." He pulled the notebook from his pocket. "According to that certificate, Sara Delaine Martin was born to June and Albert Martin on June 25, 1972, in Los Angeles, California."

"The same year I was born! She's only two months older than I am! Wait a minute. June Martin didn't leave Briar Creek until September 1972."

"Exactly. We know June Martin isn't really her name. We know the real June Martin who's registered to that social-security number was from Los Angeles and died in 1969. I'll check first thing in the morning, but I'd be willing to bet Ginny that Sara Martin's identity belonged to somebody else, too. Maybe the whole Martin family was killed in a car wreck and some con artist sold their identities as a package deal."

"Wow," Analise said softly. "This is getting really bizarre. Sara doesn't even have her own name. That feels…I don't know…creepy. Kind of sad." She halfway expected Nick to turn away in scorn at her fanciful observation, but he didn't.

"Yeah, it is," he agreed. "Sad. Sara—or whoever she really is—would have been a lot better off if her mother had given her up for adoption."

"Whoever she really is," Analise repeated. "Maybe she never had another name. Maybe she only has somebody else's identity. How awful not even to have your own name."

Nick shrugged, the gesture casual, contradicting the uncomfortable intensity that turned his eyes to a deep sapphire hue and made Analise catch her breath at this further evidence of the unexplored depths of Nick Claiborne. "I guess if you use any name for long enough, it becomes yours, like actors or writers."

"I guess. But it's not fair that I should have everything and someone like Sara has nothing," she repeated. "Not even her own name."

Nick turned away from Analise's impassioned stare, backed out of the parking space and pulled onto the street. He had to get rid of her soon. She got on his nerves, under his skin…and inside his emotions. She made him crazy…in more ways than one. Not enough she alternated between getting into trouble then smoothing trouble in totally illogical ways. Not even enough that she had him constantly fighting an insane desire to touch her. In addition to all that, she yanked him back to old habits, to a desire to keep her out of trouble and even to care and worry about someone he'd never met…Sara Martin…because Analise cared so deeply. She was going to get both of them into a world of trouble if he didn't get her gone soon.

"Who's Ginny?"

"What?"

"You said you'd be willing to bet Ginny. Is that one of your sisters? Your mother? Your…girlfriend?"

"You could say that. Ginny's my plane."

"Your plane has a name?"

"Absolutely. She's my best friend. If I treat her right and give her enough to drink, she never gives me any trouble. She never chatters. No matter how long I leave her alone, she's always there when I get back and she never complains.''

"I see,'' Analise said slowly, and he tensed, wondering what she was *seeing* now. He didn't have to wait long. "So your sisters and your ex-wife all went off and left you after you took care of them, but your plane doesn't.''

He frowned. "Going away and having their own lives is the best thing my sisters and my ex ever did. It left me free to have my own life. Do we need to go back to the motel before we head for the airport and our respective destinations of Minnesota and Texas?''

"Well, sure we need to go back. We have to tell Horace and Mabel goodbye.''

"Do you get personally involved with everybody you meet? We had a business arrangement with Horace and Mabel, that's all. We paid them for a night's lodging.''

"It would be extremely rude to leave without saying goodbye.''

"Fine,'' he snapped. "Since you and I have a business arrangement whereby you're paying for my time, we'll do whatever you want with that time.''

That ought to put things in their proper perspective...for both of them.

Analise was silent for a few minutes, lulling him into a false sense of serenity. Just as they pulled into the Rest-a-While Motel parking lot, she turned in the seat and fixed him with that scorching green gaze.

"You must miss your sisters an awful lot. What are their names?''

"Will you get off this kick about my sisters?'' He wasn't about to tell her their names, to bring her another step further into his world. "Come on. Let's tell the Finches goodbye and head for the airport.''

Damn! She had him thinking in personal terms, *Tell the Finches goodbye* instead of *Check out of the motel.* The sooner he got her on the way back to Texas, the better. They had an hour's drive to the airport. Surely he could survive another hour without going completely bonkers...and pulling her into his arms and kissing her until she stopped talking.

"Are you still in love with your ex-wife?"

Her tentative question stopped him halfway out the car door. He turned back to face her.

She smiled and fluttered her hands. "Sorry. I didn't mean to get so personal. Just forget I asked. It's none of my business. I—"

"No," he said. He hadn't intended to answer that question either, but somehow the denial slipped out as if he'd wanted to be sure she knew. Probably it was only because he couldn't think of any other way to stop her chattering. "I'm not sure I ever was really in love with her," he continued, feeling compelled to explain now that he'd let her con him into opening up the subject. "She was completely irresponsible and I had some crazy notion I ought to take care of her."

"I see."

There she went with that *I see* business again! But before he could ask her what she thought she saw this time, she twisted in the car seat and slid out the door.

Chapter Five

Pretty amazing, Nick reflected, that they were driving a small, four-passenger car and Analise managed to cram about fifty people into it...the same group who'd flown with them last night...her mother, her father, her fiancé, her friends. To his dismay, he caught himself thinking of them as people he knew, as his friends. He caught himself listening to her stories with interest.

Analise needed to carry a warning sign: *Caution! Harmful to your emotional health.*

"As soon as we get to the airport, I've got to call my parents," she said, one foot on the floorboard and one purple-sandal-clad foot resting on the seat with her knee upraised, her entire long, golden leg demanding far too much of his peripheral vision. The car had no air-conditioning, and Nick knew he was perspiring profusely, but Analise didn't seem to be affected by the heat. She gave the truth to the tradition that Southern women didn't perspire; they glowed.

"They'll be home from church by now," she continued.

"Not that I'm all that eager to talk to them. They're not going to be happy with me, but I need to let them know I'm all right. They worry so much. I'll never forget one time when I was five. There's a creek that runs through town…that's why they call it Briar Creek…and it has lots of blackberry briars. Anyway, my friend, Linda, and I were down by the creek, playing pirates and eating blackberries, and we found this cave. It was cool, out of the sun, and we knew pirates buried their treasures in caves. We were digging diligently with a couple of arrowheads we'd uncovered when they found us."

"Who found you?" Nick asked when the flow of words stopped abruptly.

"The who-o-o-ole town. Everybody was looking for us. My dad had to sedate my mom. She was totally freaked."

"Sounds like your mother overreacted. How long were you gone?"

"I don't know. A couple of hours at most." She gave a long sigh and leaned forward, laying her chin on her knee. She'd tied her hair back with the purple scarf, and the wind from the open car windows blew the wisps about her face. "I feel like I've been on a lifelong mission to prove to my parents that they don't need to worry about me, but no matter how hard I try, everything I do makes it worse. When I went off to college in Austin, I thought I finally had it made, that they'd accept that I was grown and mature and able to take care of myself. That's where I met Richard. You know, the undercover cop who taught me to pick locks and stuff. I thought he was so glamorous, taking risks and knowing how to survive. He couldn't afford to mess up. I thought if I could only learn the things he knew, then I'd be self-sufficient and my parents wouldn't worry."

Nick wasn't quite sure how picking locks and playing poker would have made her self-sufficient, but it seemed to make a cockeyed kind of sense the way Analise told it. "I take it that plan didn't work either."

She heaved another, bigger sigh. "No. I was doing my homework, practicing what he'd taught me about hot-wiring cars...which did come in handy this morning, if you'll recall...anyway, I was practicing on my own car in the dorm parking lot, and I got arrested. I didn't have any identification with me, and they ran me in. They called Dad since the car was registered in his name, and he came and got me. My parents never had liked Richard, and it turned out in the end they were right. Going with him only got me in trouble. And then he got all upset because I'd made such a public scene and said it would jeopardize his cover, so we broke up." She shrugged. "I never learned to ride a bicycle because it scared my mother so badly, I was too nervous. When I went to college where she couldn't see what I was doing, I took up in-line skating and broke my nose. The parental units were always right."

She leaned close to him, making him dizzy with her nearness. "Can you see the scar? Dad had a plastic surgeon friend of his do the job. Mom wanted me to go ahead and get a nose job like she did. She has a tiny, perky nose now, but she's a tiny person. I like my nose. I think I'd look funny with a tiny, perky nose."

"I like your nose." He clenched his mouth shut. He hadn't intended to say the words aloud, and he certainly didn't want to say the rest that were floating around in his head. *I like your eyes and your lips and your breasts and your long, golden legs.*

"How did you get your legs so tan when your face and neck are like ivory?" Oh great! In trying to keep one set of dangerous words under control, he'd let another slip out of his treacherous mouth, admitted he'd been studying every inch of her.

She leaned back and lifted a leg into the air. He swallowed hard and tried to keep his eyes on the road ahead.

"Tan in a tube," she said. "Redheads never tan, just freckle." She lowered her leg—thank goodness—then fumbled in her tote bag and, with a flourish, produced a white tube. "This stuff is great, but it fades so fast." She flipped open the top and a vivid picture of her rubbing the goop over the entire length of her legs took control of the remnants of Nick's brain. He gulped and almost swerved off the road.

The jerking motion flung Analise against her door then back against him. Touching him, covering him with her honeysuckle scent…and her tanning goop. His foot hit the brake in a reflex action…as if he could put a brake on the escalating madness speeding through his body.

The car lurched to a stop along the shoulder of the deserted highway.

"Oh, dear! It got all over you! I'm sorry!" Analise's fingers stroked light, fairy touches over his cheek and along his neck, removing the slippery stuff and sending his blood racing and his heart pounding. This was insane! How could he possibly get turned on by some ditzy, noisy female dumping goop all over him then wiping it off?

She moved up to his hair. "Well, the good news is, you're already tan and your hair's already brown, so I don't think it'll leave dark splotches. I'm getting as much of it as I can, but you're really supposed to wash it off with soap and water."

Nick had a vision of himself with golden outlines of Analise's fingerprints burned into his face, neck and hair, visible evidence of the force he felt when she touched him.

She held her hands out, examined them then shrugged and began to smear the stuff on her own arms. "I was going to put some more on my arms anyway before you ran off the road. What happened? Did you swerve to avoid hitting an animal?''

She'd only been planning to put it on her arms?

Not that putting it on her arms wasn't a sensuous activity the way she did it, in spite of her chattering. But the thought wouldn't have sent him careening off the road, throwing her against him, throwing his whole body out of kilter.

''Oh, it's on your chest and jeans, too.''

He'd unbuttoned the top couple of buttons of his shirt in deference to the heat, and when she touched his chest, he lost the hairbreadth of control he'd had left. He cupped her chin in his hand, his fingers lying along the smooth, warm skin of her cheek, and tilted her head up to look at him. Her green eyes were wide and startled and fearful and filled with the same ache he felt, the same desire. Her lips, those lush, generous lips that had haunted his dreams, were slightly parted as if waiting to be kissed and he knew this was the only chance he'd ever have. In half an hour they'd reach the airport and she'd charter a flight back to Texas while he went on to Minnesota. If it killed him, if it pushed him over the brink into insanity, he had to have one taste of her lips.

He brushed her mouth lightly with his and she responded tentatively. It was the merest whisper of a kiss, but enough to hook him, to make him want more no matter what the cost. With a groan of surrender he returned, capturing her lips, her mouth, exploring, tasting, drinking in every swirling sensation—the softness, the firmness, the heat, the honeysuckle scent mingled with the spicy scent of the tanning goop, the impassioned way her lips moved against his, the total giving of herself, holding nothing back.

She was alive and real and he wasn't touching only her lips, only her body, but all of her…her essence, her spirit, her needs. And all of him responded in a way that went beyond his hormones, that lured him and overwhelmed him and made him want even more.

A truck rumbled past, the rush of air shaking their car, shaking Nick's brain so that from somewhere he found the strength to stop kissing Analise. Removing his lips from hers was one of the hardest things he'd ever done. Bench-pressing two hundred pounds was nothing compared to this effort.

Her eyes fluttered open, dazed and smoky green with passion.

Dropping his hand from her chin and cheek was the second hardest thing he'd ever done.

She blinked and sat back. ''I'd better fasten my seat belt in case you see another animal and have to swerve again. What kind of animal was it? Did you know that armadillos now range as far north as Missouri? I don't know if they're into Nebraska or not. I wonder why they'd ever want to leave Texas?''

Nick gripped the steering wheel so tightly his knuckles turned white. ''It's too hot to talk,'' he said, knowing that made no sense and not caring. That kiss had fired every neuron in his entire body, leaving him receptive, open to all stimulus, including Analise's chattering, which suddenly felt wonderful as it danced along his nerve endings, every word a caress.

He was crazy to have kissed her. He should have known she wouldn't be able to kiss without turning it into something personal, without a part of her bursting into him and making itself at home. He had to put a stop to this escalating madness, to any further encroachments into his life.

''Okay,'' she agreed. ''The...uh—'' She pointed to his thigh, to the blob of her tanning stuff that still rested on his jeans.

He swiped it off. ''Do you happen to have any tissues in that Mary Poppins bag of yours?''

She hesitated, giving him a strange look, then dived into her bag without a word and produced a small package.

Finally, after the longest, hottest, most tantalizing hour he'd ever spent, they arrived at the small, private airport where Ginny waited to rescue him from whatever the hell Analise was doing to him. He parked the rattletrap car.

"Let's go wash our hands and faces," she said, then turned and slid out. They were the first words she'd spoken for the last half hour.

Let's go wash our hands and faces? The comment seemed to come out of nowhere. Of course, just because his brain had been completely saturated with thoughts of that kiss and all the things it did to him didn't mean that had been the only thing on Analise's mind. His hand was still slightly sticky from the tanning goop, and she'd gotten it on both of hers as well as on his face and hair. Washing their hands and his face was a logical thing to suggest. The hair, however, would have to wait.

He followed her inside the terminal, a couple of paces behind, just enough so he had a good view of her long legs flashing with each stride, her rounded bottom moving enticingly in those purple shorts.

Thank goodness it was almost over. He was intensely relieved.

That twinge of regret that the wild ride was over, that his time with Analise was over, only made him more relieved. Her up-close-and-personal attitude was getting to him, and he neither needed nor wanted the hassle that came with those offbeat, irrational feelings. She'd already become much too real a person. He'd been incredibly dumb to think he could kiss her and then get her out of his system. That had only made it worse.

If he was around her for any length of time, he wouldn't be able to resist kissing her again, not after those mind-bending, runaway sensations that went beyond anything he'd ever experienced, that were Analise-specific. She was like a street drug, sending the user into such euphoria that he could easily forget the downside, the awful pain of withdrawal.

He needed enough distance from her to put her back in her box of client, a woman who'd hired him to give her fiancé a wedding present.

Give her fiancé a wedding present. He repeated that thought, trying to picture her in a bridal gown, gazing adoringly at another man, promising to love, honor and cherish another man.

He couldn't force himself to do it, and that sent his adrenaline surging, activating his fight-or-flight response. In this case, it had to be Analise's flight.

Analise hurried into the small airport ahead of Nick. She was upset that she wasn't going to be there when Nick found Sara. However, after that scorching kiss that she could only compare to the liftoff of an airplane but a thousand times more frightening and exciting, she knew she didn't dare be alone with him again. She couldn't wait to get back to Briar Creek and the safety of Lucas's nonthreatening friendship.

Nick definitely brought out the worst in her…made her feel things an engaged woman shouldn't be feeling, made her so nervous she chattered, telling him her entire life history as well as that of everybody she knew. He made her want to do wild and crazy things, to prove she *could* do wild and crazy things, that she wasn't irresponsible like his ex-wife, that she was every bit as competent and fearless as he was—even though she knew she wasn't, and that trying to prove it would only get her into trouble.

Another good thing about going their separate ways would be that maybe the tanning cream on the palm of his hand wouldn't get dark enough to notice until she was out of his reach. It had been half an hour since the accident, so she was pretty sure no amount of scrubbing would head off all the effects, but they needed to try.

The airport only had one bathroom.

"Go ahead," she encouraged Nick. She'd had tan palms before. Most of it would be gone before her wedding. Not that the wedding pictures ever showed palms, anyway.

The claustrophobic sensation pressed against her chest again at the thought of her wedding, making her want to go on to Minnesota or wherever with Nick no matter what the danger. Or because of it. Because he represented a life-style she'd never had, living on the edge, flying around the country, leading a glamorous existence...unafraid of anything.

"Ladies first," he said politely.

"I've got to call my parents. Priorities!" She smiled, walking backward and motioning him to the wooden door marked Rest Room.

He shrugged and went in, and she looked around for a pay phone.

This airport bore an uncanny resemblance to the one in Rattlesnake Corners, Wyoming. For one thing, no handy pay phone. At the rear of the room a portly, balding man sat behind a desk that held the only phone she could see.

"May I use your telephone?"

The balding man laid down his newspaper and looked up. "You gonna call long distance?"

Analise gazed out the windows at the countryside sparsely dotted with houses that were either really distant or really small. "Is there anybody to call who wouldn't be long distance?"

"Yes, ma'am, there's a few."

"Well, I am going to call long distance, and I have a credit card." She rummaged in her handbag and withdrew a wallet, opened it and flipped through until she found the right card. "See?"

"Yes, ma'am. You want to just tell me the numbers, and I'll dial it for you?"

She studied the man silently for a moment. He didn't trust her. Well, this wasn't Briar Creek where everybody knew her. There was something to be said for living all your life in one spot.

She gave him the sequence, one number at a time, watching as he laboriously punched in each digit, then finally handed her the phone.

And she got a busy signal. Her dad must be on an important call and had disabled call waiting.

She clenched the receiver tightly. She ought to call Lucas. He'd pass along a message. And he was, after all, her fiancé.

She couldn't. Not so soon after kissing Nick. Not until she got her head and lips cleared of that kiss and the wild euphoria it evoked.

She handed the receiver back to the man.

"Nobody home?" Nick asked, coming up behind her.

"Busy."

"Go ahead and, uh, wash your hands while I make arrangements with Minnesota."

Go ahead and, uh, wash your hands? Did he think she was using that as a euphemism? Had he perhaps not washed his? She grabbed his left hand and turned it over, palm up. It was getting tan already. She sniffed. Soap. He had washed. Maybe that would minimize some of the effects.

He slowly withdrew his hand, and she looked up to see both him and the man behind the desk watching her curiously.

Short of the convoluted truth, she couldn't come up with a single logical explanation for sniffing Nick's hand. She smiled and darted toward the bathroom.

When she came back, Nick was talking earnestly to the man behind the desk. "There's got to be something!"

"Nope," the man said.

"What's wrong?" Analise asked, suddenly fearful. "Aren't you going to be able to fly to Minnesota and find Sara?"

He turned to her, dismay, confusion and something else…anticipation?…warring on his face. "Everything's set for Minnesota. But the owner of the only charter service in the area took a group to the Northwest Territories for a two-week fishing trip and decided to stay with them." He paused, letting the import of that statement sink in. "I can't get you back to Texas from here. You're going to have to fly to Minnesota with me."

Analise froze. The image of a heavier-than-air craft lifting off the ground with no conceivable way to keep from crashing back to earth took on a whole new meaning.

She was doomed.

And she couldn't wait.

This disaster was probably going to move her trip to jail for stealing her own car out of the negative and into the positive column, comparatively speaking.

Chapter Six

Nick woke early the next morning in the small motel room in Wanitka, Minnesota. He wouldn't go so far as to say he felt refreshed, but at least the room had been cool thanks to the numerous cracks around the door and in the walls. He'd been so exhausted, he'd slept soundly in spite of troubling, arousing dreams of kissing Analise. In fact, he distinctly remembered that, even in his sleep, he'd fought against leaving the last dream because he knew that as soon as he woke, she'd be on her way out of his life.

Which was a good thing and couldn't happen soon enough.

She'd been surprisingly subdued during the flight over and the drive to the motel. Even more surprisingly, he hadn't been one bit less agitated by her silence than he had been the night before by her chattering. Her very presence set his nerves jangling...and tingling.

Especially since he'd lost his mind and kissed her.

She had a certain charm in spite of her ditziness...or maybe because of it. She needed a keeper, and he knew from past experience how susceptible he was to that disastrous trap. It was so easy to get sucked into taking care of helpless women, investing time and emotions...and for what? Kay riding away on the back of that motorcycle had been the final confirmation that he wasn't cut out for that role.

Stay loose. Keep it impersonal.

He switched on the bedside lamp and swung his feet onto the floor...and watched an entire extended family of roaches skitter for safety. Well, he'd know when Analise got up next door from the screams that were bound to ensue.

Texas had its share of every crawling, creeping creature known to science, and he'd been called on to kill at least a thousand of each species in the defense of the helpless women in his life. At least this was bound to make Analise more anxious to get back to her ivory tower in Briar Creek. She probably had maids to kill bugs for her at home.

Actually, he had to admit, accusing Analise of being a spoiled rich girl wasn't completely fair to her. She hadn't complained about the crummy motel rooms, the dilapidated cars, the greasy-spoon restaurants they'd eaten at. In fact, she'd been quite resourceful.

The memory of the resourceful thing she'd done with his car yesterday morning while he was still asleep sent him racing to get dressed and over to her room before she escaped and helped him some more.

Standing at the sink at the back of the room, he took his shaving cream from his kit and squirted some into the palm of his left hand. The poor light in the bathroom made his palm look tan, especially against the mound of white foam...which reminded him of another white mound—Analise's tanning glop.

He shook his head, smeared his face and picked up his

razor. It couldn't be. He'd wiped the stuff off his palm with a tissue.

However, he seemed to recall she'd said something about the necessity to wash it off with soap and water, and she'd been quite insistent they wash their hands at the airport.

He drew the razor along his face. Analise had opened the tube with the intention of using it in the car. She knew they didn't have soap and water. She wouldn't have done that and risked tan palms herself. It was just the poor lighting.

Except Analise didn't always plan ahead very well.

He rinsed his hand and compared both palms. The left had a distinctly dirty appearance, not at all the golden shade of Analise's legs. But then, palms weren't supposed to be tan.

That was just great. Wherever he went, people would think he had dirty hands. One dirty hand, anyway.

But it would wear off, he assured himself. Analise had said that, too, he was pretty sure. He wasn't going to get upset. It wasn't like a huge tan spot on his face.

He stared at his foam-covered face in the mirror.

Surely not. He already had a tan.

He shaved hurriedly, exposing the slightly darker streak that ran along one cheek.

Virtually unnoticeable. Just a dirty smudge.

He drew in a deep breath. So what if he looked as though he hadn't bathed lately? It could be worse. With Analise, there would always be a *worse* state that could be achieved.

He opened the shower door and heard a faint humming noise that seemed to come from Analise's room.

Nah, he was being paranoid. Old places made strange noises.

He turned on the water, setting the pipes to groaning and wailing and eventually producing a cool drizzle. He could no longer hear the humming noise next door, but he knew it was there, and the knowledge filled him with dread.

Maybe Analise had tucked a hair dryer in that bag of hers and was drying her hair, he told himself. Or a blender to make a chocolate malt for breakfast. After yesterday, nothing she did would surprise him.

Dressing hurriedly, he ventured outside and was immensely relieved to see the old gray station wagon the Minnesota airport had provided still parked in front of his room.

He knocked on Analise's door and waited. A minute. Two minutes.

The morning was deliciously cool, almost like a fall morning in Texas, but Nick could feel the sweat breaking out on his forehead and upper lip.

Where was Analise?

He knocked again. "Analise! Are you in there?"

For once he would have been thrilled to hear her say something.

He pressed an ear to the window and heard the humming sound again. It wouldn't take that long to make a malt. So much for his thoughts of a blender.

Analise had a lot of hair, but he didn't think it would take that long to dry it. His sisters had a lot of hair, and among the four of them, they'd managed to tie up the bathroom for hours at a time, but there was only one of Analise.

What if she'd dropped the hair dryer in the bathtub and was even now lying unconscious or worse?

He frowned at his own runaway imagination.

The hair dryer would have shorted out and stopped running. Wouldn't it?

Not that he was worried about her. He wasn't going to be worried about her. He barely knew her. She was his client, that's all. He had no obligation to worry about her, to take care of her.

Okay, he was a little worried, but only the way he'd be

worried about a stranger. Especially a stranger who had a proclivity for getting into trouble, a stranger whose parents worried, with good cause, when she was out of their sight.

He knocked one last time. "Analise, if you don't open up, I'm coming in!"

He took his wallet from his pocket and removed a credit card. She wasn't the only one who could perform breaking and entering.

He slid the plastic into the space between the door and frame, easing the simple lock aside and pushing in.

"Analise?" he called as he shoved open the door.

She stood at the vanity at the rear of the room, her back turned to him, clad in nothing but turquoise underpants and bra…bikini turquoise underpants. Her brilliant hair spilled onto her ivory shoulders, and the entire picture was so breathtakingly beautiful, so vibrant and alive, that for a moment he could only stare, taking in and savoring every nuance.

Just as he managed to swim to the surface of reality and order himself to close the door and leave, she lifted her head and her gaze met his in the mirror in front of her. She whirled around, her eyes wide, their green adding another facet to the Technicolor effects.

"I'm sorry," he mumbled, though she probably didn't hear him over the noise of the hair dryer she held in one hand. He backed out and closed the door then leaned against the peeling paint of the building, trying to catch his breath and stop the swirling of his senses.

A woman in her underwear. That's all he'd seen. There was no reason to go completely berserk, to feel that the image had been burned into his retinas for all time.

A woman in her underwear drying her hair.

No, she hadn't been drying her hair. It had lain softly around her shoulders.

The door swung open and she stood there wearing the

turquoise blouse and khaki shorts she'd had on the first day. Every muscle in his body tensed as he waited for what she'd say about his breaking into her room.

"Good morning," she said, as perky as ever. "Did you knock and I didn't hear you? I'm sorry. I was trying to get my shorts dry. I didn't have any more clothes with me, so I washed these, and the shorts didn't get all the way dry last night. The blouse did, but it's silk. Khaki is so thick. Especially the seams. They're still a little damp, but it's probably going to be hot today, so that may work out all right."

It was a relief to hear her chattering again, put their relationship back into the proper perspective. She chattered and he got annoyed. He could deal with that much better than worrying about her...infinitely better than the image of her sleek body in that turquoise underwear.

Still, he had to admire her for washing out her clothes, not even complaining that her shorts were still wet.

"Are you ready to go find some breakfast?" he asked.

"Sure. I'll just get my bag." She turned back inside and walked across the room. A roach darted under the bed.

"I hope you weren't upset by the bugs," he said, inviting her to complain, to remind him of her weaknesses, give him a reason to push away that flash of admiration.

"Bugs?" She threw her bag over her shoulder and came back to the door.

He indicated the faded brown carpet where the roach had appeared then disappeared. "The roaches. That's a hazard of staying in old buildings. They're always around."

"Oh, the cockroaches. They're not bugs." She closed the door behind her and looked up at him. "That's a fallacy most people buy into. The order of bugs is like the squash bugs, bedbugs, mealybugs, that sort of insect. Cockroaches belong to the Blattaria or Blattodea order. And they've got a bad reputation undeservedly. There's no proof they carry disease, they don't sting or bite, they're an important link in the food chain and they play a major role in the decomposition of decaying matter, especially in the woods and places like that.''

"What?" Good grief! She sounded like a college professor. She opened her mouth to answer his question, but he lifted a hand to stop her. "No, never mind." He started for the car but turned back. "Is that some kind of trivia that you picked up for a game or something?''

"I'm an entomologist. Well, I would be if I dared leave home and go to Dallas or Houston or somewhere that's looking for an entomologist. But since nobody in Briar Creek has any interest in the study of insects, I work at the library. I minored in library science.''

Analise, the scholar. Analise, an entomologist. Analise, a library worker.

Analise, the quintessential contradiction.

"Your parents won't let you leave home." She'd more or less told him that before, but he'd been eager to ascribe her decision to immaturity, to an unwillingness to work, to another facet of her ditzy persona.

A longing filled her eyes and she looked more sober than he'd ever seen her. "They would. But it's not worth it to make them worry so much. When I was away at college, Mom called every day. She wouldn't be able to handle it if I moved. I know she's being paranoid, but it's because she loves me. And Dad feels the same way. He hides it better than Mom, but I can tell. They're the most wonderful parents in the world and making them happy is more important to me than being an entomologist." She turned away and strode over to the car, waiting for him to unlock the door.

Well, damn. It was getting harder and harder to maintain a safe emotional distance from Analise. Maybe she'd pull a bag of chips out of her purse and munch noisily all the way to the restaurant. He could pretty well count on the fact that she'd chatter some more.

Maybe she'd mention her fiancé again.

That thought was a mental slap upside the head.

Analise was his client, she was unpredictable and undependable and flaky and annoying, and she was engaged. Those elements were certainly heavy enough to outweigh anything else, including her vitality, her zest for life, her gentle spirit and his libido.

If for any reason they couldn't locate a plane for her to charter today, he'd fly her to Minneapolis and put her on a commercial airline. If he lost so much time on that task that he didn't complete the case before her wedding, well, that was her problem. She should have thought of that before she flew up and disrupted everything.

One way or the other, she'd be going back to Texas today. He could maintain for another hour or so.

She turned to him, her head tilted to one side quizzically, and he realized he'd been standing on the sidewalk for several moments while she waited beside the car. "Did you lose your keys?" she asked. "Do you need me to pick the lock?" She smiled that delicious smile of hers and he could feel himself sinking into it.

He lifted his hand, brown palm toward her, reminding himself that she was a walking catastrophe. "How long before this stuff wears off?"

She stepped closer and took his hand in hers. "Two or three or four days," she said, the words seeming to come from far away, barely audible over the wind roaring in his ears at her soft, hypnotic touch. "If it's any consolation, I have two." She exhibited them, and for no good reason he wanted to laugh...laugh and kiss her tan palms that had felt so soft on his skin.

Maybe he could maintain for another hour or so.

* * *

Perched on a stool at the counter of the small restaurant in downtown Wanitka, Analise nibbled on the remains of her cinnamon roll and watched Nick at the pay phone across the room. With the distance and the other customers talking, she couldn't hear his words and she didn't even need to. He had his back turned to her, his shoulders in the faded denim shirt square and determined. Nick was extremely capable. He'd find her a way back to Texas today.

And nothing would please her more than to get home to the safety of Briar Creek, of her parents, of her comfortable relationship with Lucas.

She fidgeted on the counter stool, trying to figure out why Briar Creek no longer felt safe and Lucas no longer felt comfortable. It had to be better than here.

She couldn't believe she'd spouted all that data to Nick about cockroaches. Such a blatant attempt to impress him. She was totally humiliated. Especially considering that he'd walked in while she was in her underwear. The worst thing about that was, rather than wanting to run and hide, she'd wanted to stand straight, to suck in her stomach, to throw back her shoulders…to do everything in her power to make herself attractive to him. She'd even shoved away an errant wish that she'd been wearing her Miracle Bra.

Nick had such a tempting air of danger about him, an air that consistently lured her into proving she wasn't afraid. Like the time when she was eight years old and her friend Marilyn had dared her to climb into the open boxcar of a freight train. Her efforts at being daring had ended her up in Tyler, calling her parents to come get her. They were not pleased.

Nor had they been pleased when she'd brought Richard home, explaining that he had to keep his hair and beard long and dress in an unkempt fashion to be an effective undercover cop. That trip down Danger Lane had ended her up in jail for breaking into her own car…and her parents had to come to bail her out.

Nick wasn't an undercover cop and the things he did as an investigator were not, she knew, as dangerous as what Richard had done. Nevertheless, he had that same aura of superconfidence, of daring and defiance, and she was real sure her parents wouldn't be pleased to know she'd kissed him, been seen in her underwear by him, and couldn't seem to stop thinking about him.

Nor was Lucas likely to be pleased that his fiancée was fascinated by another man so close to their wedding.

That thought shoved a weight against her chest and made her mouth dry.

"Could I have another cola?" she asked the waitress with orange hair piled atop her head in a complicated arrangement of curls.

"Sure, hon." The woman took the glass, scooped in more ice and held it under the cola spigot. "Don't look so sad," she said as the liquid fizzed in. "Your man's not going to leave you." She set the drink in front of Analise and removed their breakfast dishes.

"Oh, he's not my man! He's a private detective I hired to find somebody for my fiancé. I mean, not exactly *somebody for* my fiancé. For his father, actually. I mean—" Analise made herself stop chattering to this stranger. She smiled and shrugged. "It's complicated."

"Life always is."

"Some parts are worse than others, though."

The woman…Hazel, according to her name tag…smiled and wiped the counter. "That's a fact, hon. Especially when there's a man involved. We redheads seem to attract trouble."

Analise sipped her cola. "I think I'll dye my hair."

Hazel laughed. "Won't do you a bit of good. I was a blonde when I met my fifth husband, Pete, the guy that owns this place. Actually, my hair's kinda white now unless I color it. But Pete said he saw the redhead under the blonde and now under the white. So I do it red for him, but you can't find anything in a bottle that looks natural like yours does. You got pretty hair.''

"Thanks. My grandmother on my mother's side was a redhead. My mom's a blonde, though, and my dad has brown hair. Guess that's why they feel like they have a changeling for a daughter.''

"Your folks from around here?''

"No. My family's been in Texas forever. I'm just up here with Nick looking for someone.''

"Who you looking for? I've lived here all my life. I know most people in these parts.''

Analise brightened at that. "A woman named June Martin. She's short, has brown hair, kind of nondescript and she'd be in her early fifties by now. She has a daughter named Sara who has red hair like us, and she'd be about my age.'' Hazel shook her head, but the movement was slow and uncertain. "They came here in 1979,'' Analise persisted, latching on to that flicker of uncertainty, hoping to stir the woman's memory. "When Sara was seven. They probably lived out away from other people. June was a tough, demanding parent. Sara was a quiet, downtrodden child.''

Hazel frowned thoughtfully.

Nick slid onto the stool. "Okay, Analise, we're all set. I'll fly you to the airport in Minneapolis in time to catch a flight this afternoon.''

Analise nodded. "Good. I'm glad. That's great.'' It was good. It was great. And if she had any sense at all, she'd be glad. This empty, desolate feeling must be that red hair making her weird. "Hazel, could I have another cinnamon roll?'' That ought to take care of the empty part.

"Sure thing, hon. I make these myself, every morning.''

She lifted a plastic lid, took out another large pastry oozing butter and plopped it onto a plate.

"No kidding! They're fantastic."

"How about a little more coffee, Nick?" Hazel asked.

"Uh, yeah, thanks."

She filled his cup then moved down the counter to other customers.

"Hazel? Nick? Have you ever been around anybody for more than five minutes without becoming their best friend?" Nick grumbled, sounding angry when he should be happy. He was getting rid of her. He should be ecstatic. That's all he'd wanted from the first moment they met.

She studied his angry profile as he lifted his cup. He gulped the coffee then made a face. "Awful stuff. Bilge-water."

"You liked the first cup just fine," she reminded him. "And in answer to your question, yes, there is someone I've been around for more than five minutes without becoming friends. You."

He lowered his cup and looked at her, obviously stunned at her words.

She looked back at him, just as stunned. "N-not that you should be my friend," she stammered. "I'm your client. Business relationship. You're doing a good job. We don't have to be friends. No point in it since I'm leaving today. This afternoon. On a plane. Back to Texas." Why didn't something stop her? Where was a lightning strike or earthquake when you needed one? "Not that we're enemies, of course."

"Business associates," he said firmly. "Not friends, not enemies, just business. Nothing personal." He swigged the rest of the coffee he'd reviled a minute ago and slid off the stool again. "I'll go make some phone calls, check on that birth certificate and see if I can get a local address for June Martin. Take care of business."

"Good," she repeated. "I'm glad. That's great." She took another bite of the cinnamon roll that had suddenly become dry and tasteless.

"Hazel, can I have some quarters?" Nick asked.

Hazel came back down to their end of the counter. "Sure thing, hon." She accepted his dollars and returned a handful of change then watched him cross the room to the phone.

Analise ducked her head and took another bite of her pastry, but she felt the weight of Hazel's gaze return to her. *He's not my man,* she wanted to say, but her mouth was full.

"These Martins," Hazel said, and for a moment Analise thought she was talking about birds. "Are they your relations?"

Analise shook her head and dared to look up since Hazel apparently wasn't going to discuss Nick's behavior after all.

"I was talking to Gladys and Hank." She tilted her head toward a middle-aged couple at the other end of the counter. "They built a new farmhouse back in '79 and rented their old one to some people that may be the ones you're looking for."

Analise straightened, her attention focused. Had she found June Martin and Sara?

"I don't know how I could have forgotten that child even for a minute," Hazel continued. "I was married to Louis back then—my second husband—and we had the grocery store over on Sycamore Street. Sara was such a quiet, shy little thing, scared to death of that mother of hers. I used to give her—Sara, that is—candy and gum and such like. Her mother never bought anything but the basics and you could sure tell she didn't like me giving her daughter stuff. She never said anything, but you could see it in her eyes. She'd just clench her teeth and not say a word, like she didn't want to cause trouble or draw attention to herself. Louis always said there was something going on with that woman we didn't know about.''

Analise's hopes slowly fell. "You're speaking in the past tense. Does that mean they don't live here any longer?''

Hazel shook her head. "Gladys said they only stayed two or three years then they moved out in the middle of the night.''

"Oh. Could I have another cola?''

"You sure can, hon.'' Hazel scooped in more ice and refilled her glass. "That little Sara sure did like cola. Every time I'd offer her a pop, those big green eyes would light up and she'd always choose a cola.''

Analise turned the glass, feeling the cold against her fingertips, watching the pattern of condensation rings on the countertop, straining to focus on a half-seen, just-out-of-reach pattern to the saga of June and Sara.

"Is that why you thought they might be my relatives?'' she finally asked. "The red hair and green eyes?''

"Partly. But it didn't click until your guy called you Analise. Sara was always wagging around a ratty old doll with red hair. The only time I ever saw her stand up to her mother was one day when June tried to take that doll away from her. She didn't argue or anything, just ducked her head and hugged that doll as tight as she could. June finally gave up. Like I said, she never wanted to make a scene. Anyway, one time I asked Sara what her baby's name was, and she said it wasn't her baby. It was her sister, and her name was Analise. Such a pretty name and real unusual. I wrote it down so I could use it for one of my kids. 'Course, I never had any kids. 'Scuse me, hon, I see Luther looking my way. I better get him some more coffee.''

She said it wasn't her baby. It was her sister, and her name was Analise.

Analise was glad Hazel had left her alone for a moment.

She was so stunned, she couldn't think of a thing to say. Even her talent for chatter had left her.

She'd had a make-believe sister named Sara and, later, a red-haired doll named Sara.

Sara had a red-haired doll she designated as her sister and named Analise.

Nick slid onto the stool next to her, ran his fingers through his hair, heaved a long sigh and rested one elbow on the counter. "The birth certificate's a complete phony. It's not on file in Los Angeles. It's not even on a proper form. The hospital doesn't exist. Brick wall. We're back to square one as far as figuring out who Sara's father is, and I couldn't find any current records on June. They must have moved on again. Where'd your waitress friend go? I need some more coffee."

"Do you believe in spiritual sisters? Spiritual twins?"

"Huh? Spiritual twins? I've got twin sisters, but they're completely physical. If they weren't, they wouldn't have been able to borrow my sweatshirts and return them with nail polish all over the front or put a big scratch in my new car or—" He stopped and frowned as if he suddenly realized he was telling her family secrets he hadn't intended to divulge. Must have been a pretty boring family if that's the best he could do in the way of secrets.

"That's not what I mean," she said, and repeated what Hazel had told her. "Remember I said I felt some sort of connection to Sara? That I was meant to find her and—" She spread her hands in a gesture of helplessness. "I don't know. Find her and even the scales or something. Now do you believe me? Doesn't this prove something?"

Nick listened attentively, but he didn't appear impressed. "Analise, you're getting carried away. Calm down and think about this logically. It's been close to twenty years since Hazel talked to Sara. Her doll was probably named Lisa or Annie or Lisa Anne. Then Hazel heard your name today and got confused. There's nothing spiritual or psychic about it. At best, even if the girl did name her doll Analise, it's just a coincidence.'' He peered down the counter. ''But if those two were her former landlords, I need to talk to them.''

''*We* certainly do,'' Analise agreed.

His jaw clenched. A tic started in the tight muscle. He threw up his hands. ''Okay,'' he said. ''Fine.''

He probably was not going to be pleased when she told him she wasn't returning to Texas today. She had to find Sara. Too much was happening to ascribe it to coincidence. She was supposed to find Sara. She was being led.

That was the only thing affecting her decision to go with Nick. It had nothing to do with that claustrophobic feeling she got every time she thought about her wedding, and certainly had nothing to do with the way Nick's kiss had made her feel.

Chapter Seven

"Oh, Nick, this is terrible!" Analise leaned out the car window as they drove up the overgrown road to the house where June and Sara Martin had once lived.

He parked the station wagon beside Gladys and Hank Nelson's pickup in what must have once been the front yard. The house was pretty dilapidated, leaning to one side with a broken window in front, the porch missing a step as well as several boards.

"This place has been vacant for nearly twenty years. I'm sure it wasn't this bad when they lived here."

Analise gave him a one-eyebrow-lifted look then slid out of the car, tramping gamely through the overgrown weeds in her turquoise sandals. He followed, stopping beside the Nelsons to survey the place.

"We haven't done much upkeep on it since those people moved out," Hank drawled.

"Be honest," Gladys said tartly. "We haven't done a darned thing. Tried for a while to rent it again, but nobody wanted to live out this far. Everybody wanted to be in town and have central heat and cable television. We used it some for storage 'til the roof started to leak.''

Analise crossed the porch slowly, almost reluctantly, it seemed. Completely unlike her normal exuberance. She hesitated at the door, tracing a finger down the two rusty dead bolts.

''It's not locked,'' Hank told her. ''June put those dead bolts on. We never had a key to them.''

Analise pulled on the knob. It came off in her hands. Reaching into the hole with two fingers, she tugged ineffectually.

''Wood's probably warped,'' Hank said. ''I'll get a crowbar out of the truck.''

Nick climbed carefully onto the porch and stood beside Analise.

''Gives you a strange feeling, doesn't it?'' she asked, her words so faint he had to lean closer to hear. ''Being at a house where they actually lived. Can't you almost see little Sara on this porch, playing with her doll in the shade, out of the hot sun, and June coming to this very door and opening it and calling Sara inside to eat dinner?''

He could see the picture she painted, all too vividly. He could feel the slight clinch in his stomach at the idea of the quiet child living the unhappy life everyone agreed she'd had. And he didn't like the feeling. Getting upset about something that couldn't be changed was a waste of energy. All it did was leave him…upset. ''Analise, you can't undo the past. Why get all concerned about it, especially the past of somebody you don't even know?''

Her chin jutted out and up, but before she could speak, Hank returned with a crowbar. They pried open the door and went in.

A couple of mice scuttled across the floor, nimbly avoiding several holes, and disappeared into the wall. Cobwebs festooned the small living room like sad, dirty party decorations. Myriad animal tracks marred the thick layer of dust, and rotted boards left holes, exposing the earth beneath. The place had a musty, deserted smell.

Though he stood at least a foot away from Analise and could only see her from the corner of his eye, Nick could feel her tensing as she looked around.

"It was clean as a whistle when they moved out," Gladys said, as if she, too, felt Analise's concern. "I never did like that June Martin, but she was a good housekeeper and a regular churchgoer and she always paid her rent on time."

"I thought she skipped out in the middle of the night," Analise said.

"She did, but she was paid up for another two days when she left. I reckon they packed that old trailer they came in and hauled out of here. They didn't have much furniture. I offered them some old things we had, but she didn't want them. Strange woman. Kept to herself. People are friendly around here, but she wasn't having any of it. Put on those two dead bolts and nailed all the windows shut."

"Okay if we look around?" Nick asked before Analise had a chance to tell these people exactly why June Martin kept to herself…and, in the process, her own complete life story and probably most of his, too.

He couldn't imagine they'd find any clues in the old house. Anything June had overlooked would have decomposed or been destroyed years ago.

"Sure. But watch your step. Floor's pretty rotten."

Nick started off but stopped when he realized Analise wasn't following him. That shouldn't bother him, he reminded himself. It was what he wanted, wasn't it? To get back to his job, alone? To leave her behind?

He came back and took her arm to draw her with him…not because he wanted her with him and not because the house gave him the creeps but just because she looked sort of lost and frightened, gazing around the place almost as if she were in a trance.

"First bedroom's where June stayed and the second was Sara's," Gladys called after them, then, more softly, she spoke to her husband. "Let's go back outside and wait. This place makes my skin crawl."

Nick made a move to stop at the first door, but Analise tugged away from him and went straight to Sara's room. She stopped in the doorway and gasped, one hand over her mouth, her eyes wide.

Flashbulb images of everything from a dead body to mismatched window hangings flipped through his imagination as he sprinted to her.

In the middle of the room, a skunk with tail upraised regarded the visitors from bright, speculative eyes.

"Don't startle him. Just back up real slow." Nick grasped her waist and urged her away from the door.

The skunk darted through a hole in the floor and disappeared, and the terrible tension burst like an overinflated balloon.

Analise broke into laughter and turned to him, swiveling without dislodging his arm, creating an entirely different kind of tension. He wasn't sure when or how his other arm went around her. Apparently his body parts had declared independence from his brain and taken off on their own. He'd never have allowed that to happen if he'd been in control.

But, oh my, she did feel good nestled there, looking up at him, her eyes sparkling, the laughter fading, leaving her lips parted in a half smile.

She lifted one hand and trailed her fingers along his cheek, and the sensation was exquisite, her touch soft like butterfly wings yet scorchingly erotic. Several other parts of his body took off on their own...his heart racing wildly, his blood rushing to regions below his waist where her body pressed against his.

"It left a streak," she said breathlessly.

He had no idea what she was talking about, but he wasn't going to ask, couldn't find the words to ask since his brain had ceased to function, abdicating total control to his body. Maybe not a wise surrender but certainly a pleasurable one.

Analise was almost positive she hadn't intended to fall into Nick's embrace. It was just that she'd become so immersed in ferreting out the secrets of the old house, she'd forgotten to avoid him. His arms around her were strong and sure, and she felt wonderfully safe even as her adrenaline soared. The combination was provocative and delectable.

But this *wasn't* safe, she reminded herself. She slid her hand away from the brown streak left on his cheek by her tanning cream, down to his chest so she could push away from him.

Dark hairs peeked from the open neck of his faded denim shirt, and somehow her hand forgot its mission and strayed to tangle in those hairs, to touch the firm, warm skin beneath.

He groaned and pulled her closer and she realized that wasn't the only thing about him that was firm. The knowledge that she excited him, the feel of him pressed against her, combined to push her over the edge, out of the plane without a parachute, intoxicated by the thrill with no fear of the eventual crash landing.

She moved her hand from its place on his chest, from the distance it kept between them, sliding it up to his neck...and the diamond on her finger flashed a warning.

Lucas's diamond. The symbol of his trust, of their engagement, of her determination to do something right for a change.

NO RISK, NO OBLIGATION TO BUY...NOW OR EVER!

GUARANTEED

PLAY "ROLL A DOUBLE" AND YOU GET FREE GIFTS! HERE'S HOW TO PLAY:

1. Peel off label from front cover. Place it in space provided at right. With a coin, carefully scratch off the silver dice. Then check the claim chart to see what we have for you – TWO FREE BOOKS and a mystery gift – ALL YOURS! ALL FREE!

2. Send back this card and you'll receive brand-new Silhouette Romance® novels. These books have a cover price of $3.50 each in the U.S. and $3.99 each in Canada, but they are yours to keep absolutely free.

3. There's no catch. You're under no obligation to buy anything. We charge nothing – ZERO – for your first shipment. And you don't have to make any minimum number of purchases – not even one!

4. The fact is, thousands of readers enjoy receiving books by mail from the Silhouette Reader Service™. They like the convenience of home delivery...they like getting the best new novels BEFORE they're available in stores...and they love our discount prices!

5. We hope that after receiving your free books you'll want to remain a subscriber. But the choice is yours – to continue or cancel any time at all! So why not take us up on our invitation, with no risk of any kind. You'll be glad you did!

THIS MYSTERY BONUS GIFT
WILL BE YOURS __FREE__ WHEN
YOU PLAY "ROLL A DOUBLE"

SEE CLAIM CHART BELOW

315 SDL CQWS

215 SDL CQWG
(S-R-07/99)

YES! I have placed my label from the front cover into the space provided above and scratched off the silver dice to reveal a double. Please send me all the gifts for which I qualify. I understand that I am under no obligation to purchase any books, as explained on the back and on the opposite page.

Name: _____
(PLEASE PRINT)

Address: _____ Apt.#: _____

City: _____ State/Prov.: _____ Postal Zip/ Code: _____

CLAIM CHART

🎲🎲	**2 FREE BOOKS PLUS MYSTERY BONUS GIFT**
🎲🎲	**2 FREE BOOKS**
🎲🎲	**1 FREE BOOK**

CLAIM NO.37-829

PRINTED IN U.S.A.

The Silhouette Reader Service™ — Here's how it works:

Accepting your 2 free books and mystery gift places you under no obligation to buy anything. You may keep the books and gift and return the shipping statement marked "cancel." If you do not cancel, about a month later we'll send you 6 additional novels and bill you just $2.90 each in the U.S., or $3.25 each in Canada, plus 25¢ delivery per book and applicable taxes if any.* That's the complete price and — compared to the cover price of $3.50 in the U.S. and $3.99 in Canada — it's quite a bargain! You may cancel at any time, but if you choose to continue, every month we'll send you 6 more books, which you may either purchase at the discount price or return to us and cancel your subscription.

*Terms and prices subject to change without notice. Sales tax applicable in N.Y. Canadian residents will be charged applicable provincial taxes and GST.

BUSINESS REPLY MAIL
FIRST-CLASS MAIL   PERMIT NO. 717   BUFFALO, NY

POSTAGE WILL BE PAID BY ADDRESSEE

SILHOUETTE READER SERVICE
3010 WALDEN AVE
PO BOX 1867
BUFFALO NY 14240-9952

NO POSTAGE
NECESSARY
IF MAILED
IN THE
UNITED STATES

If offer card is missing write to: Silhouette Reader Service, 3010 Walden Ave., P.O. Box 1867, Buffalo NY 14240-1867

This time she did push back from Nick, and he released her. She spun around, drawing in deep breaths until the world stopped spinning, until she was again in the hallway of the dusty old house instead of somewhere in outer space, dancing among the stars.

Nick was silent, but she knew he was there behind her. She could feel him as surely as if she were still touching him.

"All my life," she said, striving to keep her voice steady, "I've taken risks and done things that scared me in order to prove that I could, that I wasn't afraid, and because of the rush that comes with facing danger and surviving. I know I've hurt my parents by worrying them, but never intentionally. I always think they won't find out until it's over and everything's fine and they'll see that there wasn't any need to worry in the first place. I've never knowingly hurt anybody or betrayed anybody and you make me want to betray Lucas who's never been anything but a wonderful friend to me." She paused as she realized what she'd just said. "That didn't come out right. I didn't mean he's *only* a friend. I meant—" She swallowed hard. "I like Lucas a lot. I respect him. I admire him. I—"

She swallowed again. Why couldn't she bring herself to say she loved Lucas? She'd told him that lots of times. For years she'd told him that.

In the same way she told her other friends, her female friends, that she loved them.

Without any of the passion she felt for Nick.

But she'd known that all along. Wasn't that why she'd agreed to marry Lucas? No passion, no *rush*, no danger…no problems. Safety. Security. The right thing to do.

She heard Nick's footsteps as he walked away from her, felt his presence leaving her. "Let's have a look inside June Martin's room," he said as if their encounter had never happened.

Maybe it hadn't for him.

But even as she thought it, she knew better.

Nick felt the chemistry between them every bit as much as she did.

Her life hadn't always worked out exactly the way she'd wanted, but she'd always known what she wanted. Her goals had been clear if sometimes unattainable.

Until this trip.

Until she met Nick.

Until Nick kissed her.

Suddenly everything around her was confusing and complicated and her wants were contradictory. She wanted to make her parents happy, stop their worrying about her, and she could do that by marrying Lucas.

That would make her happy, too, of course. No more dancing with disaster.

No more kissing Nick.

No more incredible, wildfire sensations when he touched her.

She should let him take her to Minneapolis and catch that flight back home, the way he planned.

Squaring her shoulders as if walking into battle, she entered June Martin's old bedroom, deliberately focusing on finding the woman, avoiding all thoughts of Nick.

"If they left anything here," Nick said, "it's been gone a long time."

Analise wrapped her arms around herself and nodded. "It's just a dirty, empty room with holes in the floor, like the rest of the house."

"What did you expect? A cold chill? Psychic vibrations?"

She couldn't answer. That was pretty close to what she'd expected.

Nick peered through the open door of the small closet.

"Not even a clothes hanger left." He stepped inside and looked up. "Lots of cobwebs. What's this?"

At those words, Analise darted into the closet beside him, her shoulder brushing his, her gaze turned upward to an attic opening. A bit of stained fabric hung through a crack where the board that covered it had been moved to one side.

"Analise, get out of here. You're going to get filthy."

"I can always take a bath if I get a little dirty. It's not a terminal condition," she snapped. Any minute he'd probably get around to "Be careful, watch your step, look both ways before you cross the street, don't run with a stick because you'll poke your eye out."

"All right. If that's what you want." He shrugged and reached up to push the cover all the way off the opening.

Dirt, dust and other particles she didn't care to examine too closely sifted down, followed by a larger object, the source of the remnant of white. Nick caught it.

An old doll with a once-white dress and red hair.

She took it from him and stepped back into the light of the bedroom, brushing off the debris and examining the doll closely. That portion of the roof apparently had no leaks and the cool, dry air in the attic had preserved the doll amazingly well.

Nick followed her. "Analise—"

"Yes," she whispered, a deep, black sadness swirling from the darkness of the attic and permeating her soul. "I think it is. It's Analise, Sara's doll."

"Probably," he agreed.

"What was it doing in the attic above June's closet?"

"I don't know."

She looked him directly in the eye, and his gaze slid away. If he didn't know the answer, it was because he didn't want to. "You're a detective," she said. "I'm only an entomologist pretending to be a librarian and I can figure it out. Sara loved that doll. June tried to take it away from her in Hazel's store, but she couldn't do it in public. She didn't dare make a scene that might attract attention to her since she was a thief. So she hid it and they moved away, leaving Sara's doll behind. That woman is evil!''

Nick wrapped his arms around her and pulled her close. She tried to resist but had neither the physical nor the emotional energy. Laying her head against his solid chest, inhaling the soap and denim scent of his shirt, felt so good, so comforting. It was completely different from his embrace of a few minutes ago.

''Don't do this to yourself,'' he said, stroking her hair. ''This Sara is a stranger, someone you don't know and may never know. You can't be responsible for her pain. You're getting yourself all worked up for nothing.''

''You're right.'' But the pervasive sadness wouldn't go away. She shook her head and backed out of his arms. ''No, you're wrong. Logically, you're right, but this isn't about logic. I do know Sara.'' She pressed the doll to her heart. ''In here, where everything that matters comes from.''

''Where everything that hurts comes from,'' he said quietly.

His comment startled her. He'd never before admitted to even a nodding acquaintance with pain. She stared at him, trying to get past the shadows in his gaze, to read his mind…his heart.

He turned away. ''I'm going to check out the kitchen. We've got a lot of miles to travel today.''

Not as many as he thought, but this probably wasn't a good time to tell him her decision to continue with the search instead of going home. More than ever, she needed to find Sara Martin. She knew it was pure fancy, but she almost felt that Sara was waiting for her, expecting her to arrive at any minute. And that's what she was going to do. Find Sara and return her doll to her.

All she had to do was stay away from Nick, not touch him, not look at him, not think about him, not dream about him at night.

She could do that.

She *had* to do that.

They searched the rest of the house and found nothing except more dust, dirt and mice. When they walked back outside to join the Nelsons, Analise stepped off the porch and drew in a deep breath, filling her lungs with fresh air, the clean smell of grass and earth in summer, a faint whiff of clover...of freedom. Only then did she realize how trapped she'd felt inside. Were there psychic vibes in the old house after all, left from so much sadness? Was she somehow able to tune in to Sara and feel the way Sara had felt...trapped in that house with her evil mother?

Hank eased himself away from the tree trunk he'd been leaning against and ambled over. "What've you got there? A doll? Where'd you find that?"

"In the attic." Nick dusted off his jeans and shirt.

"As though it had been deliberately hidden there," Analise added.

Gladys shook her head and clucked. "I'm not a bit surprised. That little girl carried that doll with her everywhere. I've come up on her a few times in the yard here talking to it just like it was a real person. That Martin woman didn't like that one little bit, I can tell you. She didn't want her daughter to have anything to do with anybody 'cept her, not even a doll."

"Did they leave any kind of forwarding address?" Nick asked. It was the right question, but it was also a change of subject from Sara and her problems back to business. He seemed to have a talent for doing that. Sometimes, she had to admit, it worked out for the best.

Like every time the two of them touched.

But Sara had become something other than business to her. When they found her, Sara would need a friend.

"Like I said, moved out in the middle of the night," Hank replied to Nick's question, but Gladys's forehead wrinkled in thought.

"I do seem to recall that she got a letter from some bank after she left. I kept it a long time, waiting to see if we'd hear from her and I could forward it, but we never did."

"Do you remember which bank?" Analise asked excitedly.

"Oh, honey, it's been a lot of years ago, and my memory's not what it used to be. Seems like it might have been Ohio or Idaho or one of those short states with a lot of i's and o's."

Analise's hopes wilted.

"Any chance you might still have that letter?" Nick asked.

"I'm sure I threw it out years ago."

Hank draped an arm around his wife's shoulders. "I wouldn't be so sure about that. If you kids want to ride over to the house with us, we'll look. Gladys never throws anything away. She's got every picture our kids and grandkids ever drew for us, every letter they ever wrote us. She even saves those letters from Ed McMahon."

Gladys pushed Hank's shoulder. "Oh, stop that. You like to read our kids' letters over and over as much as I do. And I do not save those contest letters. Just the ones that say to keep the number in case. But now that I think about it, could be I put June Martin's letter up somewhere and forgot about it. If you two want to follow us home, I don't mind checking a couple of places. Give you a chance to wash up. I see you both got something all over your hands."

Nick shot Analise a meaningful glance then looked down at his palm.

Good grief. Was he going to throw that little accident up at her forever?

She started toward the car. He came up behind her.

"I don't suppose I can talk you out of taking that ratty old doll with you."

"Nope."

"I didn't think so."

He hadn't even tried to argue with her. That was a good omen for their impending trip together to that state with all the vowels.

Analise pulled up in front of a convenience store less than a mile from the small airport in a town half an hour from Minneapolis. Nick had flown her there, seen to it she had a rental car to get her to the commercial airport in Minneapolis and then gone into the office to file his flight plan or whatever it was pilots did in those little buildings.

He'd been so pleased when Gladys found the old letter to June Martin offering her a job with a bank in Choctaw, Iowa, that she hadn't wanted to bring him down by telling him she was going with him after all. Fate had given Sara's doll into her safekeeping and that proved she was supposed to find Sara.

She dashed into the convenience store and replenished her supply of junk food then hurried back to the car.

A tidal wave of guilt washed over her as she noticed the row of pay phones outside the store. She hadn't called home since Saturday. She had plenty of valid excuses...no time, no phone, a busy signal. She'd reassured her mother and Lucas on Saturday and told them she wouldn't be home for a few days...but, in the interest of complete honesty, she had to question whether she was deliberately avoiding talking to her parents and Lucas.

This trip wasn't going exactly as she'd planned. Rather than returning in triumph with good news for Lucas, proving once and for all that she was competent and reliable, she was bouncing around the country, *off on another tangent,* her folks would say, flirting with the danger of being attracted to another unsuitable, tempting man. If she really wanted to show herself to be competent and reliable, she'd get away from him as fast as she could.

But she couldn't back down just yet. She had to find Sara.

She had to prove that she could withstand the temptation that was Nick...prove it to her parents, to Lucas and to herself.

If nothing else, riding in a plane so much was helping her overcome her fear of flying. Part of it was probably that she'd come to trust Nick. He could be a major pain, but he was competent, in control of his life and everything around him. If he thought he could fly the plane safely, he could.

She pulled out onto the highway and floorboarded the gas pedal. If she didn't get back to that plane before Nick did, she'd have to drive all the way to Iowa.

Nick strode briskly across the tarmac toward Ginny. Amazingly, Analise hadn't murmured one word of protest when he'd put her in a rental car and sent her to Minneapolis to catch a commercial airline back to Texas. He'd expected to have a fight on his hands, especially after the emotional way she'd behaved upon finding that doll.

She was setting herself up to be hurt. When they found Sara Martin, she wasn't likely to welcome her mother's accuser with open arms. Analise was too emotional, too open, too impetuous. She let herself get involved too easily, set herself up to get knocked down.

As he neared the plane, an inexplicable reluctance slowed his steps.

What the hell was the matter with him? He was glad Analise was gone. He was thrilled to be alone again.

He shoved aside that odd, empty feeling somewhere in the vicinity of his heart, the same strange feeling he'd had every time one of his sisters left his life. He'd even felt that way when Kay left.

But he wasn't involved with Analise. He couldn't be feeling empty because she was out of his life. Maybe he had heartburn from all the rich, greasy food they'd been eating in restaurants, not to mention her unending supply of junk food.

He'd feel better once he got back into the air, into the glorious solitude of flying. He could immerse himself in the complications of solving this case now without interference from Analise's chatter, her emotions that overflowed and spilled onto everybody around her, including him, her vitality and exuberance...

He dismissed his errant thoughts, did his preflight checks, strode up the wing and swung open the door to his plane.

"Déjà vu!" Analise leaned out, a wide smile stretching her lush lips.

Chapter Eight

They were barely a hundred miles into Iowa when the storm came up...hard and fast with no warning. Analise gave a strangled cry when they hit the first turbulence and then was blessedly silent even with lightning flashing all around them and thunder rumbling loudly.

Actually, she'd been pretty quiet most of the flight.

When he'd opened the door of his plane to find her waiting inside a second time, he'd been furious. Not so much with her as with himself for being so happy she was there. Against every ounce of intelligence he'd thought he possessed, he'd allowed her to babble and bubble her way under his skin. Every minute he spent with her was only going to make it that much tougher when she left to marry that Lucas person in Texas.

What was it with him? Was he some kind of masochist...drawn to capricious women who were just passing through his life?

Of course, she hadn't known he was angry at himself more than at her, and he hadn't told her. It wouldn't have helped anything.

As soon as the storm hit, he radioed the nearest small airport and diverted their course to land there. It wasn't far, but the winds were strong and unpredictable and the rain was blinding. It took all his concentration to keep the plane under control.

Though the landing was a little bumpy with the low visibility, he felt everything went as smoothly as could be expected under the circumstances. He taxied to a stop then turned to Analise and found that she'd gone quite green.

"It's okay," he assured her, wanting—against all common sense—to pull her into his arms and comfort her. For someone who feared flying, she'd held up pretty good. "We're safe."

She fumbled with the door handle.

He reached for her arm to restrain her. "We'll sit here and wait it out. There's no point in trying to get to the office. It's pouring rain!"

She threw off his arm, opened the door and crawled out.

He had no choice but to go after her.

The rain pelted him with cold, stinging intensity.

Analise stopped a few feet away and bent over. The intermittent flashes of lightning gave an eerie, strobing effect to her slim figure. He ran to her and wrapped an arm about her.

She sucked in deep, noisy breaths for a few moments, then straightened and lifted her face to the rain. Finally she wiped the water from her eyes, turned to him, lifted that determined chin and marched regally back to the plane.

"Are you okay?" he asked when they were both inside with the door closed...and both dripping water all over the custom interior of his plane.

She nodded, her teeth chattering.

He produced a brown army blanket from the back and wrapped it around her shoulders.

"I was so scared! I thought we were going to die," she

finally said. "The lightning was everywhere and we were bouncing all over the place and the plane started down and the needle on that gauge over there was spinning around so fast I thought it was going to fly off and we were going to crash right into the ground. But we made it! You did it!"

For no conceivable reason, she was making him go all soft and mushy inside as she sat there with her pale face, big smile, wide eyes and wet hair, wrapped in that ugly, scratchy old blanket. "You were very brave."

She shook her head. "I was terrified." A flash of lightning exploded around them while thunder boomed simultaneously. A gust of wind rocked the plane, and Analise shuddered.

"You may have been frightened, but you didn't show it. You didn't get hysterical. You stayed calm until we were on the ground. That's real courage. Anybody can stay calm if they're not scared."

"But after it was over, I almost passed out. I almost lost my lunch."

"We didn't have any lunch."

"No wonder I didn't lose it. Hey, that explains why I got so upset. I must be starving." She sniffed at the blanket. "This thing smells."

"It's wool. Wet wool does that."

She shrugged it off and squared her shoulders. "Scratches, too. I don't need it." She hauled her bag into her lap and began to dig around with both hands while peering inside. One hand brought up her hair dryer.

"Sorry. No electricity except outside."

"What?" She looked at the appliance, then laughed.

With the other hand she pulled out a large bag of cheese crisps. "Hold this." He complied, and she reached in to bring out one red can of cola, then another. "I got these before we left this morning, so they're probably not very cold, but we'll need something to wash down the cheese thingys.''

He accepted her offerings. What the heck. He was hungry, now that she mentioned it, and they were stuck in the middle of nowhere until the storm abated.

Just as he was stuck with her. She'd made that crystal clear.

He'd feel a lot better, less like he was sticking his head in a guillotine, if he could summon up more irritation at the prospect.

For a few moments they crunched wordlessly, the sound almost drowned by the pounding rain which showed no signs of abating. The main thrust of the storm had passed, however, with the thunder and lightning more distant now. Visibility was zero, and the overall effect was kind of like sitting in front of a fire at night in a cabin in the woods, safe and warm, just the two of them, while the elements pounded futilely outside.

A little too cozy, but nothing he could do about it at this point.

The cheese ''thingys'' were surprisingly good. He'd have to stock up on them for the future...the future when Analise wouldn't be around to provide them.

''Do you think we'll find June and Sara in Iowa?'' she asked, taking another handful of the snack and giving the bag to him.

''Not if June holds to her pattern. She's been moving every two or three years, which could mean we have a long way to go.''

''I don't really understand that. Okay, she stole twenty-five thousand dollars, which was a pretty substantial sum in those days. But she was in the clear since she framed Lucas's father. She stayed around long enough to see that he took the blame and then disappeared because she was pregnant. I understand why she had to leave town, but why keep running? All she had to do was check the newspapers to be sure no new evidence had surfaced. In Briar Creek, that would be front-page news. So why is she so totally paranoid? Why does she think she has to keep on the move like somebody's after her?"

Nick leaned back in the seat. "I've thought about that. Admittedly, she's over the top in her reactions, but obviously the woman's a nutcase. You'd be surprised how people carrying around a load of guilt act after a while."

"I guess." Analise started to draw her knee up, then looked down at her sandals. "Oh, no! I've gotten your plane all muddy!"

Nick cringed but made himself reply casually, "It can be cleaned." And it could. He'd been through enough of his sisters' messes to know that everything was cleanable. It couldn't always be repaired or glued back together, nor could stains always be removed, but it could be cleaned. With any sort of luck, which he hadn't had lately, nothing would be stained or broken in the plane. He wasn't so optimistic about the likely damage to him that Analise would leave behind, damage that couldn't be cleaned away and wouldn't fade as easily as the tan palms.

Analise pulled off her sandals then drew her knee up, planted her bare foot on the seat and wrapped her arms around her leg. How come he'd never before noticed how sexy a foot could be, slim with long, straight toes, a high, graceful arch?

The cheese snacks in his mouth were suddenly dry. He gulped some of the lukewarm cola to wash them down.

"Anyway, I've been thinking," Analise went on. "Why did June go to all that trouble of getting a phony birth certificate for Sara? Wherever she had her baby, she could have given the doctor any name and he'd have put it on the birth certificate. They don't make you produce a driver's license ID if you're in labor, do they? Even if they did, by that time she had ID to prove she was June Martin.''

He shrugged, trying to follow her train of thought and ignore her leg and foot and the movements of her lips as she talked.

"So my point is, do you think it's possible she used that money to buy Sara? You know, black-market babies and all that?''

He shook his head. "No, of course not." He frowned. "Well, I hadn't thought about it, but I suppose it's possible.''

"That would explain everything...the money, the phony birth certificate, the paranoia, the lack of a father... everything!" She threw her arms wide and turned to him with a triumphant smile, obviously very proud of her deductive reasoning.

"It would," he admitted. "It would also explain where Sara got her red hair and green eyes, since it wasn't from her mother." A really far-out, totally insane thought hit Nick from out of the blue...or the red and green, as it were.

Analise's parents were overly protective of her. Not in the same way as Sara's mother, but they were different people, more loving people, so of course it wouldn't be the same way. They had lots of money and could buy whatever they wanted. They'd wanted children, more than one, from the sound of things, though they'd only had the one. Add to that the fact that Sara and Analise both had red hair and green eyes and Analise had some sort of bond with Sara.

He recalled the eerie connection his twin sisters had, as if the splitting of that single egg in the womb had been purely physical and they still shared the same soul. If one fell on the sidewalk outside and skinned her knee, the other, upstairs watching television, would cry and clutch her knee and know instantly that her sister was hurt. They could go shopping separately and buy the same dress. Of course, they rarely did things separately. Even now they shared a dorm room at college and were pursuing the same major, taking all the same classes.

Was it possible that Sara and Analise were twins, both adopted?

"What?" Analise demanded.

Her question startled him out of the peculiar path his thoughts had taken. "What what?"

"Why are you staring at me like that? What does that strange look on your face mean? What are you thinking that you're not saying?"

He studied her for a long moment. With no makeup, with her wet hair barely starting to dry, she looked every iota the vulnerable, insecure, eager-to-please person he'd come to know. And he couldn't shake her up even more by giving voice to some cockeyed theory that might make her question her entire world.

"Nothing," he said.

She searched his eyes, her gaze so intense he looked away for fear she'd read every thought he had...even the ones about her sexy foot.

"Damn it, Nick!" She plunged into her bag again.

"What are you going after now? A gun?"

She grinned, one hand still inside the bag. "Let's just say, something to persuade you to talk."

He'd been kidding, but suddenly he wasn't so sure. She was from Texas, and some of the daintiest Texas women had been known to pack. Analise with a gun would be a national disaster!

She jerked her hand out and he ducked. "Chocolate-chip cookies with two kinds of chips!" She burst into laughter, the sound magical in the small cabin, like petals drifting gently down from a peach tree when the wind blows in spring.

He had to stop these thoughts. How was he going to

spend more time with her in this *itty-bitty plane* when everything about her grabbed him? Her lips, her breasts, her legs, her foot, her laughter.

He wanted her. Badly. All of her. He wanted to make love to her, hold the length of her body against his, let himself dissolve in her essence, absorb her loving, laughing spirit into his.

Slowly her laughter trickled to a halt as a smoky desire darkened her eyes, dilating the pupils. Perhaps she had been able to read his thoughts after all.

She looked away from him and ripped open the bag of cookies. "These are my absolute favorites." She pulled out two. "I could eat the entire bag all by myself. Of course, it's a small bag. Don't you wonder why they put some things like really good cookies or really good ice cream in such tiny cartons? I mean, if it's really good, you'll want to eat more of it, so the size should be bigger, not smaller. Doesn't that make sense to you?"

She chattered when she was nervous. He knew that about her, just as he knew so many other things about her.

He grasped her hand that held the cookies. "Relax." She gazed at him, awareness flowing between them. He had only two options...make love to her right there in the plane if it were physically possible. Or get things out in the open, void their desire by holding it up to the light of day and examining it.

"We're both adults," he said. "We don't have to give in to this attraction between us, but we've got to discuss it if we're going to be together the rest of this trip. We've got to stop ignoring it. If we admit the feeling and get it out of the way then we can quit being uncomfortable with each other." Nick felt very mature as he spoke the words even though he suspected they made about as much sense as Analise's babblings.

He took a deep breath and turned loose her hand. He

couldn't do this if he was touching her. "I'll start. I'm—"
He cleared his throat. "I'm very attracted to you, so
strongly that it's hard to ignore the urge to touch you and
kiss your lips and..." He cleared his throat again. "But I
know you're engaged and I promise to keep my hands and
my lips to myself."

He waited expectantly, reflecting that his desire to hear
her say how much she wanted him was probably not as
mature an attitude as he'd have liked.

"I, uh—" Analise studied the two cookies she held in
her hand, trying to decide if the best course of action would
be to stuff both of them into her mouth at once rather than
risk telling Nick how she felt about him. She wasn't sure
his suggestion was the wisest way to handle things. It
seemed a little like her tendency to play with fire, but what
did she know?

"When Lucas and I first started talking about getting
married...well, when we very first started talking about it,
we were just kidding. But then we agreed it didn't sound
like such a bad idea. My folks wanted it and Lucas would
do anything for my dad. When Lucas's father got sent to
prison, the whole family left Briar Creek and went to live
in Huntsville so they could be close to his father. Lucas
was just a little kid. All his life he was shunned, first in
Briar Creek even before the bank embezzlement. His dad's
family is Native American and had different customs. Then
his dad got into trouble in high school for trying to steal
that stupid tuxedo."

She knew this wasn't what Nick had meant, but she had
to tell things in her own way.

The cookies were starting to crumble so she paused long
enough to eat them, then offered the bag to Nick. It was
the first time she'd dared to look at him since he'd told her
how he felt, since she'd begun to try to tell him how she
felt.

He wasn't laughing at her, not even inside where people sometimes laughed while they tried to stay serious on the outside. A lot of people didn't take her seriously, but Nick did.

He accepted a cookie. "Thank you," he said.

She drank the last of her cola and turned her gaze to the rain swirling down the windshield. "Anyway, Lucas's family was ostracized in Huntsville, too, since the father was in prison. After he got out, they moved to Pennsylvania. But Lucas came back to Texas. He had to prove he could fit in where it was the hardest. My dad helped him get through medical school and then took him into practice. Dad was on the bank's board of directors when the money was embezzled, and he always believed Wayne Daniels was innocent. So Lucas adores my dad and vice versa. I think my parents always planned for Lucas and me to get married. Lucas is everything I'm not. He's calm and dignified and stable and responsible. We decided if we got married, it would make everybody happy. My parents could stop worrying about me because they'd know Lucas would take care of me, and they'd have a son. He'd be a member of the family."

She picked up the bag of cookies then put it down again. She had to get through this without eating, drinking or chattering. This was too important. She had to do it right. She had to make Nick understand.

And she had to understand.

"I've never really kissed Lucas. Not the way I kissed you." She clasped her hands in her lap, then turned them over to expose the tan palms. "It's better that way." Was she talking to Nick or to herself? "Once I get all impassioned about something, once my adrenaline starts flowing, that's when things go wrong. My brain disconnects, and I do really dumb stuff and—" She flung her arms as wide as she could in the tiny space. "Chaos."

Nick grimaced. "I know all about chaos. I lived with it from the time my dad remarried when I was ten until a couple of years ago when my short-term wife rode away on the back of a motorcycle with a man she met in her pottery class."

Was he comparing her to his ex-wife? Analise didn't think she liked that. Especially because she sensed the comparison had some validity. Well, she wasn't that flaky. She wasn't leaving Lucas for any potter on a motorcycle. Nor any detective in an airplane.

"What happened when your dad remarried?" she asked, choosing the safer topic.

"My mother died when I was two, so all I knew was the way Dad and I lived. We hung out, did guy things, ate sandwiches and frozen dinners, played baseball, watched sports on TV. When I was ten years old and he married Ruth with her two little girls, suddenly the house had to be clean even if we weren't expecting company. No more eating in front of the television, not that it mattered because *Sesame Street* replaced football. Then nine months later, twins. Chaos."

"What are your sisters' names?"

He hesitated, and for a moment she thought he was going to change the subject, the way he'd done when she'd asked before. "The older two are Sharon and Becky, and the twins are Peggy and Paula."

"Where are they now?"

"Sharon's married and living in Houston. She's expecting a baby any day now. Becky's just graduated from law school at SMU in Dallas, and the twins are in college in Austin."

"Do you see them often?"

"No, of course not. They're scattered all around the state. They have their own lives now."

"So? Just because we add new people to our list doesn't

mean we don't love the old ones anymore. You didn't stop loving them when you married what's-her-name, did you?''

"Kay. Her name was Kay. And of course I didn't stop loving my family."

"You see? Just because we love somebody else, just because the people we love aren't always in our physical presence doesn't mean we stop loving them. Have you been avoiding your sisters because they left home and you think they don't need you? That's just dumb. How about your dad and your stepmom? Are you avoiding them, too?''

"I'm not avoiding anybody!"

"Don't shout at me."

He clenched both fists. "I'm not shouting. And I'm not avoiding anybody, either. Our lives change. Dad has Ruth, Sharon has her husband and the baby on the way, Becky has a new job and new friends, and Peggy and Paula have college. Kay has her motorcycle man or his replacement. I have my calm, ordinary life back, just the way I like it."

"Well, your life may be solitary, but *calm* and *ordinary* aren't words I'd use to describe it. You take chances. You track down criminals. You fly a plane out of the storm."

He shrugged. "Today was unusual. Detective work is boring and routine most of the time. I do a lot for companies checking on employees' backgrounds, spend a lot of time at the computer. Most of it's painfully tedious."

She thought about that. Actually, she had to admit, it wasn't that he led such a dangerous life, not the way Richard had as an undercover cop. It was the way he made her feel that was dangerous, the excited, out-of-control way he made her feel.

The rain was slowing and the sky was brightening, opening them up to the world again.

"So," he finally said, "we're in agreement. What's a few hormones between mature adults? We have our lives the way we want them. You'll marry Lucas. I'll keep on the same way as before, working, flying, enjoying the peace and quiet. This attraction thing between us is sort of like—'' He spread his hands as if fumbling for the right word.

''Champagne,'' she supplied. ''One glass is wonderful. It tastes good and makes you feel good, but you can't have more than one or you're in trouble.''

''Yeah,'' he agreed, sounding relieved that she'd explained it so well. ''Champagne. Exactly.''

''The rest of our lives, that's the steak-and-potatoes part.''

''Right. Nobody can live on champagne.''

''Right.''

''Good.'' Nick began his instrument check.

''Look! It's a rainbow!''

Nick didn't want to see any rainbow. He didn't want to hear the thrill in Analise's voice, the wonder over this perfectly natural phenomenon. Nevertheless, he ceased his preparations for getting back into the air and followed the direction of Analise's finger, out his side window. ''Yep, that's what it is.''

''We're in a plane! We can fly to the end of the rainbow and find the treasure!'' She laid a hand on his arm, her eyes sparkling and her entire face glowing from a light within. The rainbow might be the focus of her excitement, but the ability to see its magic came from inside her.

She was leaving herself wide open to be disillusioned and hurt.

''Analise, you know there's no end to the rainbow and there's certainly no pot of gold.''

She turned loose of his arm and rolled her eyes. ''Of course I know there's no end to the rainbow. I understand perfectly well that it's curved because the earth is curved. And I never said there'd be a pot of gold. I said *treasure*.

I already have a pot of gold. Three or four if I want them. That's not the kind of treasure I'm looking for."

A ray of sunlight streamed through the window on her side, backlighting her, setting her hair on fire so that it matched the glow in her eyes.

"What kind of treasure are you looking for?" he asked. For a split second he wondered who'd spoken, whose voice was so husky with desire.

His. Of course.

Analise heard it, too. The sparkle in her eyes metamorphosed to a blazing fire and she looked at him with that same wonder she'd had for the rainbow.

Don't! he meant to say. *I can't handle your trust, your needs, anything about you. I can't turn loose and feel so much only to have it snatched away.*

He didn't say any of it. His body had taken leave of his brain again. He pulled her toward him, covering her mouth with his, effectively preventing him from warning her...from warning himself?

She responded, offering her lips the way she offered everything...unstintingly, with no reservations. She tasted of chocolate-chip cookies and cheese crisps and rainbows and smelled of rainwashed honeysuckle.

He pressed her still-damp body to his, feeling the cool spots become warm then hot. His hand brushed the side of her breast, a movement that only teased him, making him want so much more.

Instead, he lifted his hand to the side of her neck, sliding his fingers over the smooth skin and behind to plunge into the warm dampness of her hair.

She was alive and vital...a chaos factory, to be sure, but such wonderful chaos. She almost made him want to believe in rainbows and treasures and happy endings.

Maybe he couldn't do that, but he was forced to believe

in the reality of the way she made him feel—alive and vital and full of wonderful chaos.

She pushed away gently, taking her lips from his, and those feelings seemed to go with her.

Which was a good thing.

Even if it didn't feel so good.

"What a shame that we can't live on a steady diet of champagne," he whispered.

Chapter Nine

Analise tossed her bag onto the bed in the small motel room in Deauxville, Missouri, and sank down beside it. The room could have been a clone of the ones in Nebraska, Minnesota, Iowa and Illinois. Nick was sure right about one thing. His job wasn't always glamorous.

She headed for the bathroom to freshen up. They'd finished in Illinois early and arrived in Missouri in time to do some work this afternoon.

And a darned good thing because time was running out. It was Wednesday already. Three days until her wedding.

That thought made the walls of the small room start closing in.

She turned on the cold water and splashed her face, but the shock didn't take away the knowledge that had been creeping up on her over the last few days…that she'd come on this trip to avoid dealing with the reality of her marriage to Lucas. Somewhere in her convoluted thinking must have lurked the absurd notion that, if she did something really good, something really right, like proving Lucas's father's innocence and making it possible for his parents to come to the wedding, they wouldn't have to have a wedding.

Okay, so it didn't make any real kind of sense. So she was nuts. So what was new about that?

She might have been able to go through with marrying Lucas if she'd never met Nick. Lucas was her best friend. They got along great, always had a good time. He made her feel comfortable and warm.

Nick made her feel uncomfortable and sizzling. Nick made her want him, and not in a best-friend way.

Damn! There she went again! Chasing rainbows and buried treasure, yearning for that *rush* that always got her into trouble. Hadn't she learned anything in twenty-seven years of mistakes?

She twisted off the faucet, ran a comb through her hair and slapped on a minimal amount of makeup. The woman staring back at her from the mirror looked a little disheveled and hastily thrown together, but what the heck. Who was she trying to impress? Nick?

Ha!

Since that kiss in the airplane, they'd been deliberately avoiding each other. Pretty hard when they were together constantly. Pretty hard when some rebel part of her didn't want to avoid him. Pretty hard when she'd turn suddenly and catch him looking at her as if he didn't want to avoid her either. At least, not in a hormonal way. In all other ways, she knew she drove him crazy and that he wanted to get rid of her. Was that the way he'd felt about his ex? He'd said he didn't think he'd ever really loved her, but he must have had some reason to marry her. Hormones?

She'd finally called Lucas from Iowa, though he'd sounded oddly confused and had run off in the middle of the conversation, an out-of-character action for him. But she'd managed to tell him she was all right, asked him to pass along the information to her parents and assured him she'd be home in a day or two. She'd tried to tell him about Sara, but he'd left the phone and she'd taken the opportunity to hang up.

Come to think of it, he'd sounded strange Saturday when she'd talked to him, too. Maybe he was also having second thoughts about their impending wedding.

Or maybe she just wanted him to be.

That morning she'd called home, but her parents had been out. She'd told Annie, their maid, that she'd be back tomorrow no matter what. That would give her two days to get ready for her wedding.

She *would* marry Lucas. She wasn't going to mess that up, too.

Squaring her shoulders resolutely, she returned to the generic motel-room bed. At least this place had phones in the rooms, even a copy of the Kansas City Yellow Pages. Considerate of June Martin to have finally moved somewhere close to a city.

She flipped to the Aircraft Charter, Rental and Leasing Serv ads and began to make calls.

A few minutes later a knock sounded on the door. "Ready?"

Nick. Despite the fact that everything she did annoyed him, he'd taken on the self-appointed role of keeping her out of trouble, never letting her out of his sight. She might as well be at home.

Except nobody at home could send her hormones into overdrive the way Nick did. Nobody at home made her feel safe and daring at the same time. Nobody at home had eyes like the Texas sky just before a storm and hair that always looked as though the wind had been playing with it and shoulders to fill a doorway and—

"Ma'am?" came the voice on the other end of the phone. "Are you there?"

"I'm here."

"We'll have a plane and pilot available at 2:00 p.m. tomorrow. Shall I reserve that one for you?"

"Yes. Please."

He knocked again.

"Chill out! I'm coming!"

She checked to be sure Sara's doll was still in her bag then left the dingy little room and walked out into the bright, hot sunlight…into Nick's presence.

"Okay," he said. "If we hurry, we can just make it to the local bank before it closes."

"Sure makes it easier that June Martin never learned another occupation."

"So far. She could change at any time." He held open the door of the rental car for her to enter. At least this one had air-conditioning. A phone in the room and air-conditioning in the car. Next place they went to might even have room service.

Except they weren't going anyplace else together.

He got in the driver's side and they pulled out of the parking lot.

"This is the first time she's moved anywhere close to a city," Analise observed. "Twenty miles from Kansas City as opposed to the middle of nowhere in the other places. Maybe that means she's letting down her guard. Maybe she's even still here." She knew that was a vain hope, but couldn't stop her foolishly optimistic nature from popping up. It was probably still harboring some stupid idea of returning with June Martin in tow, figuratively speaking, and everyone being so excited about her accomplishment that her parents trusted her and Lucas was still her best friend even though she didn't want to marry him and—

"I wouldn't count on it," Nick said as if reading her mind. "At two to three years per city, we've got a long way to go." He slanted a look at her. "At least, *I've* got a long way to go. You're still planning to go back to Texas tomorrow, right? You can't miss your own wedding.''

He sounded peeved. Of course, he'd sounded peeved pretty much ever since she first met him, and it was only getting worse. And the more peeved he got, the more nervous she got, which caused her to talk more and mess up more, which caused him to get more and more peeved.

"I chartered a flight for tomorrow afternoon. Kansas City to Tyler where I left my car." Telling Nick made it sound so real, so final. "I won't miss my own wedding."

"Good." He swung the car into a parking space in front of the National Bank of Deauxville and slammed on the brakes, both actions so fast, Analise lurched sideways then forward…within the confines of the seat belt he'd insisted she wear since the day he'd run off the road and she'd squirted tanning cream all over him.

The day of their first kiss.

Not that he seemed to remember that.

But he never passed up a chance to mention his tan palm even though it was only spotted now.

Together they entered the bank.

Nick pointed her toward a row of beige chairs. "Wait there while I go talk to the personnel director. Don't move. Don't leave. Don't talk to anybody."

"I have to give you credit. You were certainly right about one thing…in Wyoming, when you said you were only going to get crankier."

He sighed and ran a hand through his tousled hair. "I'm sorry, okay? It's just that—" He shook his head. "Never mind." The look he gave her reminded her of the ones she got from her parents any time she was leaving their immediate sphere of influence. But there was something else in Nick's eyes, too. Before she could figure out what, he walked away.

She strolled over to the chairs he'd indicated. The matronly woman behind the information desk looked up and Analise smiled at her. Surely smiling was an acceptable activity.

The woman's brown eyes widened, her lips curved into a huge answering smile and she leaped up from her chair. "Sara!"

Analise whirled toward the door, fully expecting to see Sara Martin walk in. Okay, Sara was a common name, but she was the dummy who still believed in treasure at the rainbow's end.

The woman charged around in front of her and grasped her hands. "I almost didn't recognize you! Look at you! Got your hair cut, wearing eyeshadow and shorts! You've always been such a pretty girl but now you're beautiful!"

Analise's head spun as she tried to comprehend what the woman was saying.

"Are you all right?" the woman asked, then frowned. "Did you get bad news about your family? Come sit down. I'll bet I know what'll perk you up! A cola in a red can!" She winked as she steered Analise toward the chairs Nick had indicated.

Analise sat down, her power to stand leaving her along with her power to speak.

Another coincidence, her brain insisted, that Sara drank the same kind of cola as she did. As for the mistaken identity, this woman hadn't seen Sara in a long time—eight or nine years if June stayed true to her pattern—and the combination of red hair and green eyes caused the error.

The woman patted her hand and bustled away. As Analise looked around the room in confusion, a couple of the tellers smiled and waved. Analise returned the greetings automatically. She was, after all, a Texan, and Texans were friendly, even to strangers.

The first woman returned with a cold cola and handed it

to Analise. She accepted the drink gratefully and lifted it to her lips for a long gulp.

"Now tell me what happened when you got to Texas."

Analise choked on her drink, collapsing into a fit of coughing.

The woman took the soda and patted Analise on the back. "Oh dear, oh dear! I didn't mean to bring up something bad. Are you going to be all right? Somebody help!"

Strong arms yanked Analise up out of the chair, wrapped around her from behind and squeezed her abdomen painfully. The air rushed from her lungs in a sudden whoosh.

"Are you okay?"

As she straightened and turned, Nick's face appeared in her blurred vision.

Trying to catch her breath, she glared at him. "Broke...my...ribs!"

"You were choking!"

"I...was not!" She drew in a deep breath. "Okay, I was choking. Now I'm...bleeding internally."

A middle-aged man with thinning hair and a trim mustache stepped from behind Nick. "Sara, we didn't expect to see you back so soon! Mr. Claiborne, you were asking me about June Martin. This is her daughter, Sara. Sara, this gentleman is interested in your mother. We were just discussing his reasons for wanting to know, when we heard Kathryn's call for help."

Analise looked at Nick. He appeared as astonished as she felt. Two people had just made the same mistake. Maybe more if you counted the tellers who'd waved. When added to the coincidence of hers and Sara's dolls, the whole thing sent an eerie chill down Analise's spine.

"Mr. Hodges, this isn't Sara," Nick said. "This is my client, Analise Brewster, the woman who wants to find June and Sara."

Hodges laughed nervously, as if not quite certain Nick wasn't making a joke. "You're not Sara?"

"No, I'm not."

The woman—Kathryn—stepped back and shook her head. "This is incredible. You could be her twin. Your hair and eyes are exactly the color as hers. You have the same nose, you're the same height." Her gaze dropped to Analise's feet. "June used to complain because she had such a hard time finding shoes for Sara. She acted as if Sara had deliberately grown unusual-size feet." She lifted her eyes to Analise's. "She wore a nine narrow."

"So do I," Analise whispered. She took the soft drink from Kathryn and downed half the contents.

"Could I see some identification?" Hodges requested.

Analise fumbled in her bag, withdrew her wallet and flipped it open to her driver's license.

He studied it carefully, then passed it to Kathryn, who gasped and covered her mouth with her hand. She and Hodges exchanged confused glances.

"Do you have a picture of Sara?" Analise asked.

Kathryn nodded slowly, went back to her desk, selected a framed picture from the half a dozen sitting there and returned.

"This was a surprise party for my twenty-fifth anniversary of working here," she said, extending the picture to Analise. "That's Sara in the background."

Analise stared at the image, herself among strangers, caught in a moment she didn't recall because she hadn't been there. Her head whirled with the eerie sensation. She spun around to show the picture to Nick. "Does she look as much like me as I think she does?"

"Yes," he said quietly. "With your hair pulled back and no bangs, that could be you. I can see why these people made a mistake."

"That's the only picture I have," Kathryn said. "June

didn't believe in pictures. If she'd ever noticed Sara was in this one, she'd probably have destroyed it.''

"Why?"

"I don't know," Kathryn replied. "I always thought it might be that she was scared Sara's father, whoever he might be, would find her and want parental rights or something. But then we found out—'' She stopped and stared at Hodges as if for direction, for permission to continue her sentence.

"Perhaps we should step into my office," Hodges suggested. "Kathryn, why don't you come with us? If anyone needs assistance, Jane or Susan can handle it."

Nick placed a steadying arm around her waist as they crossed the room and entered Hodges's office. The older man closed the door behind them.

Analise and Kathryn sank into the two visitor chairs while Nick stood and Hodges sat behind the desk in a large chair, his arms folded across his chest. "Why don't you tell me what's going on here? Are you a relative of Sara's?"

Nick folded his arms, too. His chest was much wider than the bank manager's and he wore a denim shirt and jeans as opposed to a suit and tie. He was miles ahead in the intimidation factor.

"Why don't you tell us where June and Sara are, and we'll just talk to them?" Nick said. "Cut out the middleman."

Kathryn and Hodges exchanged glances.

"Sara's in Texas," Analise said, recalling Kathryn's assumption that she'd returned from there. "She went to Briar Creek, didn't she? That's why you were so shocked when you saw my driver's license."

Kathryn nodded, twisting her hands in her lap. "Sara—'' She hesitated and again looked to Hodges. He compressed

his lips and gave a quick shrug as though he had no an-
swers.

Kathryn drew in a deep breath. "About a year ago June
Martin took sick. Come to find out, she needed a kidney
transplant. Sara, sweet girl that she was, offered to donate
one of hers, though I'm sure I have no idea why, considering the way that woman treated her."

"June was a good employee," Hodges said.

"She was a mean person."

Hodges didn't contradict her, and Kathryn continued.
"Anyway, when the doctors ran the tests to see if she was
a match, they found out Sara wasn't even June's daughter."

"I was right! She did buy Sara!" Analise exclaimed.

"Buy her? Well, she adopted her. She told Sara that her
real mother was some poor woman whose boyfriend was
rich and refused to marry her when she got pregnant, so
she gave her baby away."

"Oh." She glanced at Nick. "At least that rules out
Wayne Daniels as her father. He certainly wasn't rich."

"June never would tell Sara who her real parents were.
Just said they didn't want her, and that Sara should forget
about them. After June died—"

"She's dead?" Analise sat upright in her chair then
slumped back in defeat. It would be hard to arrest a dead
woman.

Kathryn nodded. "Two months ago."

Nick had the proof of Lucas's father's innocence and that
would have to be enough. Her quest was over. It was time
to return home. There was no reason to stay any longer.
Except—

"Why did Sara go to Texas?"

"After June died, Sara found a pay stub in the lining of
one of June's old coats. All she could make out was the
name Briar Creek National Bank. Naturally she assumed
June had worked there once and it might even be the town

where her real mother lived. It was all that poor girl had. No other family, and June saw to it she didn't have many friends."

"She kept her isolated because she never legally adopted her!" Analise gave Nick an "I told you so" glance. "It wasn't just the money. She was afraid the authorities would find out about Sara."

"The money?" Kathryn asked.

"Nothing important," Nick inserted smoothly. He moved around behind Analise's chair and rested his hands on her shoulders. As though she couldn't figure out for herself that he didn't want her to tell these people about June Martin's crime.

Yet in spite of the fact that she was irritated at him, his touch created a bond between the two of them. "Go on, Kathryn. You were saying that June kept Sara from having friends."

"Well, Sara was such a sweet girl, everybody liked her, but June kept her under lock and key. She wasn't allowed to date. They moved here when Sara was a junior in high school, and I'm sure it was just so she could live at home while she went to college in Kansas City. She was twenty-seven years old and still living at home when June died." Kathryn shook her head. "Such a shame. She was so pretty. But you know that. She was the mirror image of Analise here, and I can tell by the way you look at her, young man, that you know how pretty she is."

Analise felt hot blood rise to her face. Nick's hands left her shoulders. He cleared his throat. "Did Sara work?"

"Oh, yes. At the local library."

"The library?" Analise repeated.

"Yes, she was a librarian, and a very good one. But she told me once in confidence that she wanted to study antomology."

"Antomology?" Kathryn couldn't be trying to say what

Analise thought she was trying to say. This was getting too weird.

"Ants. Bugs."

"Entomology."

"Whatever. But June wouldn't let her. So she minored in bugs and got her degree in library science. Anyway, she went straight home from that library every day. No social life at all. They went to church on Sunday and once in a while they'd go to a movie, but June thought most of the movies were wicked, along with anything else that was fun."

"But they did take those self-defense classes," Hodges interjected.

"What?"

"June Martin was paranoid. After Sara moved out, the owners of that house found five dead bolts on the front door and every window was nailed closed. June would pick Sara up at work or school or else Sara would come by here and wait for June, depending on who got through first. Sara told us her mother took her to every self-defense class that was offered in Kansas City. Apparently she was convinced somebody was going to take Sara away from her." Hodges unfolded his arms and leaned forward. "Now may I ask why you two are so interested in June and Sara?"

Before she could even open her mouth, Nick's hands descended to Analise's shoulders again. "We think Sara may be a relative of Ms. Brewster, as you noticed from the uncanny resemblance." She twisted around to glare up at him. How could he lie to these nice people? "The fact that she was adopted," he continued, "is further evidence. We really appreciate your talking to us. So, Analise, I guess our next stop is Briar Creek."

She nodded. Of course it was. June was dead and Sara had gone to Briar Creek to find her real mother. That's where she had to go.

Nick had said *our next stop,* but what he meant was *your next stop.* His job was finished. He wouldn't be going with her. Briar Creek was a small town and everybody there knew her. If Sara looked as much like her as Kathryn and Hodges seemed to think, by now Sara had heard of Analise Brewster.

Heck, somebody had probably seen her and called in to report an Analise sighting to her parents, to reassure them she wasn't in trouble or to snitch on her if she was. Her own parents had probably met Sara by now.

She wouldn't need a private detective to find Sara in Briar Creek.

Nick would be glad to get rid of her, and vice versa.

She rose from the chair, fighting a peculiar sad, empty feeling. "Yes, thank you both very much. When I find Sara, I'll tell her how kind you were and how complimentary to her."

"You tell that sweet girl how much we miss her," Kathryn said. "She made any room brighter just by being in it."

Analise smiled and squeezed Kathryn's hand. "I will. I promise."

Chapter Ten

As soon as she and Nick were outside the bank, Analise's smile died. "I need a drink," she said.

"Another cola? That last one nearly did you in."

"I mean a serious drink. Heavy-duty. A daiquiri or margarita."

Nick laughed.

"What?" she demanded.

He shook his head and strode over to open the car door for her. "Nothing. I'll see if I can find us a bar and get you a heavy-duty drink."

But when they were seated at a corner table in a dimly lit bar, Analise ordered a cola. "I think I'm going to need all my wits about me to figure this out."

Nick regarded her seriously, his blue eyes dark and shadowed in the subdued lighting. "Bring her a margarita," he told the cocktail waitress. "And a beer for me."

"I want a cola," she reiterated through clenched teeth. Even her parents didn't order for her.

"Bring both," Nick countered.

"Fine. And you can drink the margarita as a chaser for your beer."

The waitress left and Analise leaned forward. "Did you notice all the similarities between Sara and me? Remember how I've said from the beginning that there's some kind of a connection? This proves it. We even wear the same size shoe!"

Nick compressed his lips and frowned, then reached for her hand. "Analise," he said softly, "I think you're right."

She hadn't expected him to agree so readily.

"I want you to consider something," he continued. "June told Sara that her father was wealthy and couldn't marry her mother."

"Yeah." Where was he going with this?

"You and Sara look enough alike to be sisters."

"Yeah."

"You have the same interests."

"Yeah."

"Your father is wealthy."

"Yeah. No!" She jerked her hand away from him as she suddenly realized where he was going with that line of reasoning. "I don't believe you're for real! First you try to say Wayne Daniels was Sara's father and now you're accusing my father! Some detective you are! Who's next on your list? Lucas? Maybe he was a very precocious three-year-old!"

"I'm only looking at the evidence objectively."

The waitress returned with the drinks and Analise opted for the margarita after all.

She didn't want to admit it, but Nick was right. The evidence was compelling. Was it possible that Sara was her half sister? That her wonderful father had—

She set her glass down so hard some of the drink sloshed out. "No way. My red hair, green eyes, straight nose and long, skinny feet come from my grandmother on my mother's side, not my father's! Put that in your evidence and sniff it!''

Nick lifted both hands defensively. "I'm sorry. It was something we had to consider. That's what you hired me for, to track down evidence. *Sniff it?*''

"Sniff it, smoke it, eat it...whatever."

He was right, though, and he'd had her wondering for a moment, even if she wasn't about to admit it to him. "The case is solved. You don't work for me anymore. Submit your final bill.''

Nick toyed with the damp cocktail napkin under his beer. "There's another possibility you need to consider. I told you my youngest sisters are identical twins. Well, identical means just that. They look alike, they think alike, their interests are the same. Even when they're apart, it's almost like one knows what the other is thinking.''

Analise rolled her eyes. "So now you think Sara and I might be identical twins? You warned me you were going to get crankier and crankier, but you forgot to mention that on Wednesday evening you'd become certifiably nuts. Do you realize you're making me look sane?''

Nick wrapped both hands around his beer. He didn't smile. He didn't glower. He was getting scary. "You need to think about it.''

She sighed. He was trying to help. Concern creased his forehead and softened his mouth. "It's not possible, Nick. I know I wasn't adopted. Like I said, I look just like my grandmother. Well, like she looked at this age. Although I've aged about twenty years these past few days. And if I'm not adopted, that would have to mean my parents gave up a child, and there's no way they would ever do that. If they hadn't been forced to spend every second taking care of me, they'd have had another baby. They wanted one. I've overheard them talking about how sad it was I had no sister. No way would they ever give up a baby.''

But the ideas, impossible as they were, nagged at her. Was she adopted, chosen, perhaps for her natural mother's resemblance to Grandmother Paxton?

She couldn't accept the possibility but it refused to leave her head.

The murky room with its smell of recycled, refrigerated air and cigarette smoke became oppressive. She needed to be outside, in the heat, in the open, under the summer sky.

"This drink wasn't such a good idea," she said. "I want to go to the motel room."

"I haven't touched this beer. I could fly you back to Tyler tonight."

Back to her parents, who'd suddenly become strangers? Back to Lucas, who'd be her husband in three days?

"No. I'll wait for the charter flight tomorrow afternoon. You go on, though. The case is closed. No reason for you to hang around."

He studied her for a long moment, his gaze unreadable. "There's no reason for you to charter a flight since I have to go to Tyler anyway."

Spend another three or four hours with Nick in his itty-bitty plane, every fiber of her being tingling and alive with his nearness…and dreading the loss of that nearness? With any sort of luck—bad, that is—she could spend the entire night dreading the dreading she'd do on that trip home.

"I already have the plane reserved. It would be rude to cancel this late. Anyway, I have some things I need to do in Kansas City tomorrow." That wasn't a lie, exactly. She needed to eat, breathe, things like that. "Take me to the motel and I'll get another rental car in the morning. You can go on to Tyler tonight."

"Ah, what the hell. We already have those luxurious rooms rented. Might as well get a good night's rest." He threw some bills on the table, slid his chair back and stood.

She looked up at him, trying to read what was really

going on behind his veiled gaze. As usual, she had no clue. She rose and followed him out the door.

Nick couldn't sleep.

He flopped over in bed and punched up his pillow then checked the luminous dial of his watch again. One forty-five.

Typically when a case was finished, the puzzle solved, he practically went into a coma for at least one night.

Of course, this one wasn't really solved. He didn't know who Sara's parents were. He didn't know what her connection to Analise was, though he was certain of one thing. Analise had been right about that. The two girls were connected.

That was undoubtedly the reason he couldn't sleep, the unsolved puzzle. He wasn't distressed that Analise would be leaving his life forever in a few hours. She'd never been a part of his life, so how could he be distressed? She was Lucas Daniels's fiancée. Soon she'd be Lucas Daniels's wife. He'd never had her to lose.

In the room next door Analise was probably snoozing away.

He gave up, kicked off the tangled sheet and got out of bed. Maybe if he walked around awhile, got a cola and had a snack—

Good grief! Analise's habits had rubbed off on him.

He pulled on his jeans and went outside. The rental car sat parked where he'd left it. That was a good sign.

Light shone around the curtain in Analise's room. He paused at her window only to see if he heard any strange noises. A justifiable action.

All was quiet. So she was sleeping with the light on. Some people did.

He found the vending machine on the second floor. An odd red stain at the bottom of the steps leading up to it caught his attention. Blood. He'd been a cop long enough to recognize it.

So maybe somebody had a nosebleed.

He climbed the open concrete and metal stairs. Someone had spilled a soda all over them.

And at the top...a purple leather strap...torn from Analise's sandal.

He picked up the object, trying to hold the rising tide of panic at bay.

A coincidence. Lots of people had purple leather straps on their shoes, their purses, their...whatever.

He charged back down the stairs two at a time, refusing to look at the spilled cola, the blood at the bottom. He was getting all upset about nothing. He'd done it before, panicked only to find Analise drying her shorts with her hair dryer.

When he got to her door, he drew in a deep, ragged breath and knocked.

She didn't answer.

Of course she didn't. She was asleep, like all sane people. He wasn't asleep, which just went to prove he wasn't exactly sane right now.

He pulled out his wallet and extracted a credit card. All he wanted was one glimpse of her safe in bed. She'd never even know he'd been there.

His fingers trembled so badly, it took several minutes to get the door open.

Her room was empty.

He charged in, looked under the bed, in the bathroom.

The khaki shorts, turquoise blouse, turquoise underpants and bra hung over the towel rack drying, but Analise was gone.

Calm down! he ordered himself. *Think!*

But he couldn't calm down. He couldn't think. He couldn't bear to consider the possibility that something might have happened to Analise, that the sandal strap was hers...that the blood was hers.

Headlights shone through the open door, and he raced out just as a police car pulled up.

The police, blood, a broken shoe strap—

Nick stood paralyzed while his mind screamed a denial. He couldn't lose Analise! That would be more pain, more loss than anyone should be expected to bear.

An officer got out and opened the back door. Analise's legs swung out with one purple sandal dangling, the strap broken.

Nick ran to take her arm. "Are you all right? What happened?"

"I'm fine." She smiled but her face was pale, her expression distraught.

"You call me if you have any more problems, Analise," the officer said.

She turned her dazzling smile on him. "Thanks, Jeff."

Oh, well, he should have known. She and *Officer Jeff* would be bosom buddies by now. The man would probably name his first child after her.

The squad car pulled away and Analise stood on the sidewalk and waved.

Nick ran a hand through his hair in complete frustration. He wanted to grab her and shake her. He wanted to grab her and hold her close against him and never let her go, keep her out of police cars and middle-of-the-night excursions and weddings with men named Lucas. He clenched his hands to prevent them from doing either.

"What's going on?" he demanded instead. His voice was shaky, reflecting what his insides were doing—shaking, trembling, clenching. "Why were you in that police car? What happened to your sandal?"

"Jeff brought me home from the station."

"Why were you at the station?"

She turned away from him. "How come my door's open?"

He could no longer stop himself. He grabbed her shoulders to spin her around toward him...and to touch her, to reassure himself that she was still there, her skin still warm, her heart still beating, still in the same world with him.

He released her immediately, before he lost complete control and pulled her against him. "I was worried about you! I found blood and your sandal strap by the vending machines!"

She sighed, her expression telling him she'd done something he wouldn't like. "I couldn't sleep so I went to get a soft drink. I was just about to open it when some creep came up behind me and grabbed my bag."

Nick looked down to where the infamous bag hung on one shoulder. "Apparently he didn't get it."

She lifted her chin. "He certainly did not! I hit him with my can of cola and held on tight to my bag. He kept pulling and I kept holding on and hitting him and he dragged me out of that little room and over to the stairs. He said some pretty rude things, too." It was every bit as bad as he'd feared. Nick's heart constricted at the danger Analise had been in. He couldn't have stood it if he'd lost her...not that he had her. "So I don't feel one bit guilty about him falling backward down those stairs. Okay, I finally let go of the bag and gave him a shove with one foot...that's when my sandal broke...and his momentum carried him down the stairs. But if he hadn't been trying to steal my bag, it wouldn't have happened. I had the manager call an ambulance, and he's going to be fine. Just a little head wound. They bleed a lot, you know. Can you imagine? He wanted the police to arrest me for assault?"

He threw his hands into the air. "I can't believe you! Haven't you ever heard that you're supposed to let a purse snatcher take your purse? That man could have killed you!

What could possibly be in that damn bag that's worth your life?"

She glared at him in silence for a moment. "Sara's doll," she finally said.

He lost the battle with his common sense, his morals, his sanity and pulled her body against his, exulting in the solidity of her, the rise and fall of her chest as she breathed, that she was still with him and not lying dead somewhere.

"I'm glad you're all right," he whispered, then forced himself to let go of her.

They looked at each other. She made no move to return to her room and neither did he.

"I couldn't sleep, either," he finally said. "And I don't think this incident has made me any more likely to be able to. Come on, we'll have a, uh, farewell cola."

She nodded and started off in the direction of the vending-machine room. He followed, trying to stay far enough away that he wouldn't be tempted to touch her but close enough he couldn't watch her rounded rear in those purple shorts. "They gave me a soda at the police station," she said. "Policemen are like cockroaches."

"Excuse me? They gave you a soda and they're cockroaches?"

She glanced over her shoulder with a disgusted look. "No! I said they're *like* cockroaches. They've got a bad rep, undeservedly. They're really nice if you're nice to them. Cops, that is. I've never tried being nice to cockroaches because they always run away too fast. But I suppose, theoretically, it's possible."

He had no response for that last part so he ignored it. "I was once a cop."

"You mentioned learning to shoot at the academy." She carefully skirted the blood on the sidewalk and climbed up the concrete stairs ahead of him, her gait uneven as the broken sandal flapped with each step. There was no way he could not look at her bottom. "Why did you quit?"

Quit? He hadn't quit. He was still looking at her bottom. "Oh, why did I leave the force? I don't know." They reached the machine and she stopped and turned to face him and he knew he couldn't hide anything from her open, honest gaze. Not even things he ordinarily hid from himself.

He reached around her and slid a handful of coins into the machine then punched the buttons for two colas. He didn't have to ask what kind she wanted. He knew. He knew entirely too much about her for his comfort. She'd become far too real. After she was gone, every time he drank a cola, he'd think of her. Every time he saw a rainbow or the color purple or a police car.

"Want to go sit down by the pool?" she asked. "That's where I was headed before that creep came along. I find water very soothing even if it's chlorinated."

"Sure." Maybe she'd forgotten her question about why he left the police force. When someone talked as much as Analise, she was bound to forget a few things she'd said.

But of course she hadn't.

She sat on the concrete edge of the square, green-tinted pool in the middle of the motel complex, pulled off her sandals and dangled her slim feet in the water.

He wanted to join her...toss away his shoes and dive into the pool of life without reservations, the way she did it.

"How long were you a policeman?" She popped the top of her cola, the fizzing noise punctuating her question.

"Eight years."

"And?"

"And then I became a private investigator."

"No. I mean, what happened? Did you nearly get killed

when a drug bust went bad? Did your partner get murdered right in front of you and you couldn't do anything to help?''

"You've been watching too many television shows."

"Books. I work in a library, remember? I read a book just last week where the hero, who was a cop, got squeezed off the force because of all the corruption. No?" She leaned back on one elbow and gazed up at him, her expression somewhere between intense and teasing. "Your ex, Kay, left you for that potter on a cycle because her father was a cop and he got killed and she couldn't stand to be married to another cop."

"Have you ever thought about writing novels?"

"Not that either? Let me see..."

"Okay, enough! My leaving the force did actually have something to do with Kay, but only as a last-straw sort of thing. You're going to be disappointed. My reason was boring. Nothing dramatic. There was so much sadness and loss, murdered people, people whose loved ones were murdered, people who'd lost their life savings in a scam or a robbery, wives beaten up by their husbands, drug addicts, prostitutes. I did what I could, but it wasn't enough. I couldn't fix it."

"Did Kay need fixing?"

He shrugged, staring across the pool. "I suppose. Yeah, she did. She couldn't hold a job, she couldn't keep her bank account straight and was always bouncing checks, she ran her credit cards up. She needed me."

"And your sisters didn't anymore."

He gave a wry chuckle. "I give up, Dr. Freud. You've nailed me. As a matter of fact, I did meet Kay shortly after the twins left for college. I guess I just couldn't stand all that peace and quiet and lack of chaos. Anyway, we met and married and divorced all within four months. And when she left, I had to face reality. I'm no good at taking care of people. So I quit trying, left the force and went into private practice. Now most of the time I can make people happy, get them what they want. And if it turns out not to be what they wanted after all, well, I mail them a report and I don't have to see how it affects them.''

"Most of the time," she repeated, and the depth of emotion in her soft voice tugged at him, forcing him to face her, to submit to her gaze that searched his, delving into depths he didn't want explored. "Didn't get off so easy this time, did you?"

"No," he said. "I didn't. My clients don't usually insist on coming with me."

"I'm sorry."

She didn't sound sorry, and for all the pain of loss he knew was coming, right now he couldn't feel sorry, either.

"I know. You had to prove something."

She nodded. "That I could get it right for once."

"You complain about the way your parents treat you," he said, "not trusting you and all, but it's obvious they love you very much."

"Do I complain? I don't mean it to sound that way. There has never been a time in my life when I haven't felt loved. Incompetent, but loved. I just didn't want to spend the rest of my life having Lucas take over where my parents left off, worrying about me. I thought if I could do something really big for him, things would be different after we...after I...after Saturday." She sat up, looking away from him and taking a long swallow from her cola.

"Is that the only reason?"

Analise drew her feet from the water, which had suddenly turned chilly. She'd set out with the idea of penetrating the barrier Nick kept throwing up between them and now he had her penetrating her own barrier and not happy with what she found.

"No," she said softly. "Not really. Every time I think

about that wedding, it's like I can't breathe. Like major claustrophobia, even out here in the open.''

"You don't want to marry Lucas."

"I guess not." She couldn't make herself speak the denial more definitively, admit that she'd made another mistake. "But I said I would, and I don't break my word, especially not when it would hurt so many people."

"You said during that storm that your folks wanted the marriage."

"Yes, they do. They love Lucas like a son. They want him in the family. They trust him to take care of me. He's the big brother I never had. Lucas and I talked about it for a month before we finally decided two weeks ago to do it. I knew I'd chicken out if we waited very long, and he probably would have, too. That's why we had to split the rehearsal and the wedding by a week, to get the church. When your fax came the night before the rehearsal—" She pulled her knees up and rested her chin on them, continuing to gaze across the pool to the dark row of motel rooms on the other side...anywhere but at Nick. "It was like a sign. I could do something to help Lucas, and I could avoid the rehearsal."

"You can't avoid it much longer." His voice sounded faraway and hollow, as though he was already out of her life. Not that he'd ever really been in it. He'd said himself his business was impersonal. He didn't get involved with his clients in any way. She was his client. They'd shared an assignment together, that's all.

"No," she said. "I don't suppose I can." But she wasn't sure she could go through with the wedding. She'd never lied to Lucas. He was her best friend. She couldn't stand beside him in a church and promise, before God and everybody, to love him above all others. Not when she loved someone else.

She lifted a shaky hand to push the hair off her face only to discover it wasn't in her face.

Reality. That was the only thing in her face.

Much as she didn't want to accept it, she loved Nick...loved his touch, his messy hair, his broad chest, the way he looked at her, the way she felt when she looked at him, even his crankiness when she thwarted him. It was all part of the package that was Nick Claiborne, and she loved him. If he never landed his plane in a storm again, never traveled the country in search of suspects, if he became an accountant tomorrow, he would still be the most exciting person she'd ever known. She would still love him.

She had to tell Lucas as soon as possible, had to call off the wedding.

This could very well be the worst disaster she'd managed to create so far.

She'd set out to exonerate Lucas's father and bring the guilty party to justice. Okay, she'd accomplished half of that. At least, Nick had accomplished half of it. The only thing she'd done was hire Nick.

She couldn't even bring the guilty party to justice. The guilty party was dead.

She'd determined she would find Sara and right the wrongs done to her.

But Sara had found her own way back to Briar Creek, possibly to her real parents by now.

And to top it all off, Analise had fallen in love.

Yes, this was her biggest fiasco to date. Definitely made her visit to jail for trying to steal her own car inconsequential by comparison.

"Analise?"

She gasped at the sound of Nick's voice. For a moment, she'd forgotten where she was...who she was with.

"Are you okay?" he asked. "You look kind of pale. At

least, you did for a minute. Actually, you're a little flushed now.''

She waved a hand in the air. ''Terrible lights out here. They make you—'' She swallowed. Shadows softened his square jawline. Concern deepened his eyes to the shade of the evening sky back home in Texas. Lights or not, he looked wonderful, desirable, tempting.

She stood abruptly. ''I'd better get back to my room, get some sleep. Big day tomorrow. Back to Briar Creek. Things to do, places to go, people to see.'' *Lives to straighten out, chaos to create.*

He rose and gazed down at her, his forehead wrinkled in a frown. ''You sure you're all right? You've been through a lot today. First that business with Sara then somebody trying to take your purse.''

You don't know the half of it. And she wasn't about to tell him. He already thought she was a complete flake. Confessing that she was going to cancel her wedding and jilt her best friend wasn't likely to improve her image in his eyes. Probably couldn't make it any worse, however.

She gave him a thumbs-up. ''Got it all under control.''

She cast a wary eye toward the sky, fully expecting a huge lightning bolt to zap her at that incredible lie.

Chapter Eleven

After breakfast the next morning Nick took Analise to a shopping mall near the airport in Kansas City from which her chartered flight was scheduled to depart that afternoon.

"Are you sure you don't want me to wait?" he asked.

"Goodness, no! You know how we women are. It'll take me hours to find a new outfit to wear home. You go on and do whatever you need to do. I'll get a cab to take me to the airport when I finish here." She opened the door and slid out.

He walked around the car to her. She looked up at him and suddenly his world came alive. The sun shone warm on his face. A morning-cool breeze brushed his cheek. From a tree in a nearby planter, a chickadee sang its lop-sided song.

Her eyes were the essence of summer, of the earth bursting with green life, and he remembered something she'd said when they were stranded in the storm in Iowa...that we didn't stop loving people just because they weren't with us all the time.

With a burst of ecstasy followed by a sinking heart, he realized she was right. No matter if he never saw her again, he'd never forget her. He'd never—heaven help him—stop loving her. Fifty years from now, every tree, every blade of grass, every scent of honeysuckle, every breath he took would remind him of her.

He loved her.

He supposed he'd known it at least since last night when the thought that something might have happened to her had filled him with desperate panic. Maybe before that. He'd known it but refused to admit it.

She made him crazy, but he loved her in spite of it. Or maybe because of it. Because she brought laughter and freshness and vitality. She'd danced up on his blind side, distracting him with her chatter, breaking through his defenses with her magic and making him love her before he knew what hit him. He'd let himself care again when he knew loss was the only possible outcome...loss with all the accompanying pain.

"Well," she said brightly, "thanks for everything. Solving the case, I mean. And letting me come along. And landing the plane safely during that storm. I hope we don't run into another storm on the way back to Texas. That is, I didn't mean *we* like in *you and I*. You and I could run into another storm, of course, but we'll be in different planes. We could still be in the same storm, though. Except how would we know?"

Her chattering sounded like music, and he drank in every note, storing them away for the long, silent years ahead.

"Well," she said again, and hoisted her bag higher on her shoulder. "Goodbye." She extended one hand as if to shake his, then immediately withdrew it.

No, they could never part with a handshake.

But neither could they part with a kiss. If he kissed her now, he wasn't sure he'd be able to let her go.

And she was still engaged.

"Goodbye, Analise. Have a good life with Lucas."

She turned away from him. "Thanks," she whispered and ran to the mall door then disappeared inside without a backward glance.

She'd driven him crazy for almost a week and now, like a firefly winking brightly then disappearing into the night, she'd left him.

He got back in the car and slammed the door. What was the matter with him? He'd known from the beginning that she'd be going back to Briar Creek and that Lucas person…back to her real life. So what if they'd shared a couple of mind-bending kisses and a rainbow?

He'd do what he'd done when his family had broken up and gone their separate ways, when Kay had left. His dad had his stepmom, his sisters and even his ex-wife had their own lives and he'd had to find his. He'd get back to his job, to flying, to the place he'd found where he could exist comfortably, where he could avoid personal involvement and the gut-wrenching pain that came with it. Maybe it wasn't much fun living in a vacuum, but it was consistent. You gave up the highs to avoid the lows…the losses.

He'd carry on as though Analise had never happened, they'd never met, never touched, never kissed, never broken cookies together.

As he drove out of the parking lot, he checked the rearview mirror just in case she should run out of the mall, in case she'd forgotten something, in case he had an opportunity for one last glimpse of her.

He saw nothing except the cars of strangers, no familiar red hair and rounded bottom.

He headed for the nearest public telephone. Back to work. That was the ticket.

He'd called his office before he and Analise went to breakfast and left a message for his partner, Ben, to run a check on Analise. Before he got back in the air, he wanted to see if Ben had discovered anything.

Analise thought the case was finished, but he didn't. She could talk all she wanted about this business of destiny and psychic twins, but after seeing Sara's picture, he was more than ever convinced something else was going on here.

Last night he'd put forth the theory that Analise's father was Sara's father, and Analise had rejected it vehemently. If Sara and Analise were half sisters or twins and Analise was forced to accept the fact that her father had cheated on her mother or that she was adopted, he wasn't sure how she'd handle it. She was so positive Ralph and Clare Brewster were perfect and were her natural parents, she loved and trusted them so much, the knowledge could hit her hard. If it were true, she needed to be forewarned.

He located a phone he could reach from his car and placed a call to his office. His secretary answered.

"Hi, Tess. Any calls that can't wait until I get there tomorrow?"

"As a matter of fact," she replied archly. "You're an uncle."

"An uncle? No kidding? Sharon had her baby? How is she? Was it a boy or girl?" Even if he'd wanted, he couldn't stop the flood of emotions that overcame him at that news.

"Sharon's fine, and the baby's a girl." Nick leaned back, clutching the phone receiver tightly, blinking away a film of moisture that clouded his vision. Another baby girl with tiny fists that clutched around one of his big fingers, and a beautiful toothless smile. "They named her Nicole Renee."

"Nicole? No kidding!"

"Yeah, named after her uncle, in spite of the fact that he wasn't there for her birth."

Bad enough Analise had jumped him about his relationship with his sisters. Now his secretary was getting into the act. "Was I supposed to be?"

"Tom said when Sharon got into hard labor, she told the doctor she couldn't have that baby unless her brother was there. Your mom and dad and Becky, Paula and Peggy were with her, but she wanted you, too. She caused such a ruckus, Tom called me at home last night, but we had no idea how to get hold of you."

"I was working," he said curtly, but he couldn't quite avoid a slice of guilt...irrational guilt since Sharon was the one who'd left home, not him. "What hospital is she in? Call her and tell her I'll be there tomorrow."

"Will do. That's the only message that can't wait. Ben got the message you left for him this morning. He's not here right now, but he said to tell you he's on to something. Are you heading back here?"

Ben was on to something. Nick wasn't surprised, but his heart clenched for Analise. "Yeah, I'm on my way."

By the time he arrived, maybe Ben would have something definite and he could intercept Analise at the Tyler airport and break the news to her personally, soften the blow as much as he could, prepare her for what she might discover on her return home.

He hung up the phone and was on the highway to the airport when it hit him. He'd just figured out a way to see Analise again. He was scheming against himself. What he should do was send Ben to tell Analise whatever he discovered. That was the only sane way to handle this situation.

Analise's steps were slow as she crossed the parking lot toward her red sports car. Though it was late afternoon, the sun beat down with relentless fury while heat rose from the concrete. The double assault drained what little energy she had left. The day had surely contained at least forty-eight hours, all of them ninety minutes long and enervating.

She hadn't been completely honest with Nick when she'd asked him to drop her at the mall in Kansas City so she could get a new outfit to wear home. Actually, she just hadn't wanted to stretch out the time left to spend with him. It hurt too much, like pulling a Band-Aid off your arm, one slow hair at a time instead of one painful but fast yank.

She'd chosen the fast yank, called her parents to tell them she was arriving, bought a book and read in the mall for a couple of hours. Finally she'd taken a taxi to the small airport where she'd caught her chartered flight back to Tyler.

Now she had only an hour's drive to Briar Creek. One hour away from the big confession, the Big Boom. Only this one wouldn't create a new universe. More likely it'd blow this one to smithereens.

Her parents had sounded so glad to hear from her this morning. It wouldn't take her long to change all that!

She'd asked about Sara, and they'd thought she meant her old doll so she'd let it go. First she had to get her latest catastrophe behind her, then she'd find Sara…if Sara didn't hear about it and decide she should avoid somebody who walked around dribbling disasters in her wake.

And she had a few more of those to dribble before the day was over.

Mom and Dad, now that we have the church reserved and the wedding invitations out and my wedding gown altered, I've decided not to marry Lucas after all.

Lucas, dear friend, I've got good news and bad news. The good news is, I have proof of your father's innocence. The bad news is I've fallen in love with somebody else and can't marry you.

Actually, her not marrying him was probably good news,

too. Lucas wasn't in love with her. He was just trying to do what was right, as she'd been. He'd probably be relieved to have the wedding called off.

Yeah, right. He'd be thrilled to tell the whole town that his flaky fiancée had changed her mind. Everyone would roll their eyes and smile indulgently and say to each other, *That Analise!*

Maybe they could have an unwedding instead. Eat the cake, drink the champagne and celebrate the fact that Lucas wouldn't have to pay exorbitant rates for disaster insurance after all.

She slid her key into the car door and turned it, then opened the door.

"Analise!"

She stopped. Was she hallucinating Nick's voice?

She whirled around to see him coming up behind her. "What are you doing here?"

"I wanted to deliver my final report on this case in person." He held up a file folder.

"Oh." A fleeting, insane thought had spun through her overheated brain that he'd come to profess his love and carry her away with him. Of course he hadn't. Being the conscientious man he was, he'd come to deliver his final report.

And a good thing it was that he hadn't come to do anything dumb like that because she wasn't sure she'd have the strength to make the right choice and reject this latest insane urge of hers to charge into the eye of the hurricane.

He smiled though the expression in his eyes was guarded. She fought down a desire to touch him, verify that he was real. She'd never expected to see him again, never expected to feel that excited tumult all through her mind and body and soul just from looking at him.

She ought to get in her car and leave, tell him to mail his report to her. But she couldn't. It felt entirely too good to see him. She'd have to deal with leaving him a second time very shortly, but in the meantime, she was going to savor every delicious drop of being with him.

"Let's sit in the car," she said. "Get out of the sun."

She slid in and he went around to the passenger side, climbed in and opened the file folder on his lap.

"Does this involve Sara?" she asked.

"It sure does. Have you ever seen your birth certificate?"

"No, I don't guess I have. It's not one of those things you keep on your shelf of favorite things to read."

"Maybe it should be. Look." He indicated the top document.

She peered at the name of the hospital in Briar Creek, her name and date of birth, other statistics. "So?"

"Item number four."

"For plural births only? Twins?" She shook her head. "I don't understand. Is my birth certificate messed up? How'd I manage that when I was barely born?"

He pulled aside the certificate to expose the one beneath it, almost identical except for the name. *"Annabel Cassandra Brewster?"* she read. *"Twins. Second in order of birth."* She looked at him, at the gentle smile that had finally reached his eyes. "Are you telling me I had a twin sister and she died?" Surely that wouldn't make him smile.

"No. She just underwent a name change. Sara is your twin sister."

Even as he spoke the words, Analise knew with a certainty deep inside that he was telling the truth though it made no sense. "What are you saying? That my parents gave up my sister for adoption?"

"Not voluntarily." From the stack of papers in the folder, he extracted a photocopy of a newspaper story.

Brewster Baby Missing, the headline blared.

With fingers suddenly gone numb, Analise took the photocopy from Nick.

Annabel Brewster, the three-week-old daughter of Ralph and Clare Brewster, was kidnapped last night from the nursery where she slept with her twin sister, Analise.

The print blurred and a fog seemed to settle around Analise, blotting out the world. She was much too young to remember, yet she could feel the wrenching, aching loneliness. She'd spent nine months in the same womb as her sister, three weeks in the same crib, and she'd missed her desperately when she was gone. The knowledge, the pain, was as certain as the print on the page before her. Somewhere way back in her memory in a place she couldn't access but which existed nevertheless, she'd known it all along. Her mind had forgotten, but her heart remembered.

She blinked, trying to focus on the printed words before her. No demand for ransom, the article continued. Not that they expected it from the note left in the crib.

It's not fair for some people to have so much and others so little. You still have a baby and now I have one. I'll take good care of her and raise her right.

Nick handed her the rest of the stack of papers, but she pushed them back. "Tell me what they say," she whispered. "I can't read any more."

"Your mother was distraught, of course, and the whole town grieved with her. My partner, Ben, talked to several people and they all told him that after a few months, when it became obvious your sister might never be found, your father asked everyone not to bring it up in front of your mother. He thought it was the only way she could heal and put the loss behind her...focus on the child she had left. You."

"Abbie Prather. June Martin. She took my sister."

"It certainly looks that way. She disappeared shortly after the kidnapping. She lived in a trailer park outside of town where nobody would have noticed another crying baby, so she could have hidden Sara for a couple of days. From what we've uncovered, she had an abortion years before that rendered her unable to have children. Apparently she went nuts when she heard that your mother, who had a husband on the board of directors of the bank where she worked, had money and social position, now had two babies. After she left town, the police suspected her but couldn't find any trace of her. She must have planned it from the day you were born, stolen the money to buy a new identity and get away.''

''That's why June was so paranoid, hiding from everybody, teaching Sara self-defense techniques. She was worried somebody would come after Sara, that her mother and father would find her.'' A drop of water landed on the photocopy of the first news story, and Analise realized she was crying. ''My mother and father. Our mother and father.''

Nick pulled her into his arms and stroked her hair. She allowed herself to lean against his chest, to melt into the solid comfort he offered. ''It's okay, sweetheart, it's okay.''

''No, it's not.'' She swallowed back a sob. ''All those years Sara had to live with that horrible woman. All those years she was away from her family and thought nobody loved her. All those years she and I didn't get to share.''

''But you did. Just like you said. You had a connection. You communicated on a level that only people who really love each other can find. You talked to each other even if everybody else thought you only had pretend sisters. You named your dolls after each other. You were never really separated, not in your hearts. Remember what you told me? That you knew Sara in your heart where everything that matters comes from.''

She pulled away from him, dug around in her bag and came out with a tissue. After blowing her nose, she gave him a shaky smile. "Did I say that? I'm not so ditzy after all."

With his thumb, he wiped away her tears and smiled. "No, you're not ditzy. And you're not incompetent and untrustworthy. Think about it, Analise. Your parents obsessed about you all these years not because they were worried about what you'd do wrong but because they were afraid they'd lose you, too. The whole town was worried. They've always reported your every move because they cared, not because they thought you were irresponsible."

Analise leaned against the headrest and stared at the blank red ceiling of her car. "Wow. I'm going to have to think about that for a while. You mean I've never had anything to prove except that I could stay out of the way of a crazy woman? Heck, June Martin would have probably returned me the first week! Defective merchandise."

"I've been with you almost a week and haven't seen any defects."

She sat upright, surprised at his gentle words. "Then you must have amnesia. I distinctly recall that you got pretty disturbed with me at times."

He shrugged. "Maybe a couple of times. Okay, so you've got a few quirks, but no major defects." His words were gently teasing, but his gaze remained impenetrable. He studied her silently for a moment then handed her the folder. "Everything's in here. We kept copies at the office in case you lose any of it."

"Thank you," she said, staring down at the impersonal folder…as impersonal as his voice had suddenly become. "I appreciate your delivering this report in person." There. She could do impersonal, too. At least, she hoped it came out that way, that Nick couldn't hear the love and the pain that shared her heart with the wonderful news about her sister. "This is great," she said. "I can't wait to tell Mom and Dad."

"And Lucas."

"And Lucas. Of course. After all, he was the reason I started this whole search." Oh, yes, she had lots to tell Lucas.

"Well." Nick turned away and fumbled with the door handle. "How do I get out of this thing?"

She leaned over him, unable to resist stealing this one last touch. "Right here." The denim of his shirt was soft against her arm while the chest underneath was solid, and her heart accelerated to a now-familiar, double-time tempo. She inhaled deeply, absorbing the tantalizing, seductive scents of denim and danger that belonged to Nick, memorizing the feel of him, inscribing his memory on all her senses.

"Are you catching a cold?" he asked.

She sat upright. "A cold? No, just allergies." She sniffed again and crinkled her nose. "All that strange pollen in those places we went."

"I see. Well." He slid one booted foot out the open door onto the concrete. "Let me know if you need anything else."

"I will. Thanks. For everything."

"I'm glad I could help. I hope it all works out with your sister and your parents and Lucas." He swiveled around and set the other foot out the door.

"It will. Thanks. Again."

He stood, leaned down and peered in. "You're welcome." He straightened and closed the door, then leaned down again. "Analise—" His voice had an anxious edge, as though he were about to say something very important.

"Yes?" she prompted.

He gave her a tight smile and waved. "Goodbye, Analise."

"Goodbye, Nick."

He turned and strode across the parking lot a few yards,

got in a dark blue sport-utility vehicle and drove away without a backward glance.

Analise turned the key and started her car. It was getting late. She needed to get on the road to Briar Creek…back to her life the way Nick was heading back to his.

She had a lot to return to, especially now. Loving parents to whom she could give the gift of their missing daughter. Her best friend, Lucas, to whom she could give the gift of his father's innocence. And a sister she'd never met in person but had always known in her heart, to whom she could give the gift of love.

Thanks to Nick, she had an abundance of riches to return to.

She should be ecstatic.

She was ecstatic.

Well, half her heart was ecstatic. The other half was empty. Along with all the other abundance, Nick had given her the gift of experiencing exciting, wonderful, over-the-rainbow love. Of course, he hadn't returned that love. He'd walked away from her, leaving her with a hole in her heart.

But with such an incredible bounty in her life, she'd be a greedy person to let herself be sad over that one little hole.

That one wide, gaping, painful hole filled with sharp spikes and broken glass and an aching loneliness.

She wasn't going to look at that area. She wasn't going to think about the way Nick's lips had felt on hers or the way he smiled or the way his eyes could change in an instant from the clear blue of the Texas sky on a summer morning to dark and turbulent with desire.

Nope. She wasn't going to think about any of that.

She drove out of the parking lot, flicking on the air conditioner as she went to blow Nick's scent right out of her car, out of her mind.

With all the excitement in her life—good and bad—she'd soon forget about Nick Claiborne.

In a century or two.

Maybe.

Chapter Twelve

An hour later Analise pulled up in front of Lucas's house. Resolutely, dreading what she had to do, she marched through the evening dusk up the walk and onto Lucas's porch, lifted her chin and rang the doorbell.

He didn't answer even though his Mercedes sat in the driveway and a light had come on inside the house as she came up the walk. Was he ignoring her? She hadn't even broken their engagement yet. How could he be angry with her already?

She pounded on the door with her fist. "Lucas! I know you're in there!"

Almost immediately he flung open the door and pulled her into his arms. An unusually enthusiastic greeting, but at least he wasn't upset with her. Yet.

"I'm so glad you're not mad at me," she exclaimed, pushing away and looking up at him.

He stared at her, a confused, disappointed look on his face, then took a deep breath and ran a hand through his hair. "Analise. We need to talk."

She moved past him and perched on the back of his sofa. "I know! I have so much to tell you!" That was surely an understatement.

"Analise, we can't get married."

His words were as unexpected as his embrace had been, but they brought relief washing over her in huge waves. She tugged off her engagement ring and ran to hand it to him. "I knew you'd understand! I mean, you're my best friend and I'll always love you, and I know you love me like a friend, but not like—" She broke off, biting her lip. There was no point in confessing that she was in love with Nick. He was out of her life and she'd soon forget him.

"You're not going to believe everything that's happened," she continued. "I've got to talk fast because I haven't been home yet, and I know how Mom and Dad worry about me even though they shouldn't and now they won't have to."

"Wait a minute." He looked down at the ring in his hand. "You mean you're calling off the engagement?"

"Oh, dear. You are upset."

"No! I'm not upset!"

"Lucas, we don't love each other the way people should love each other when they get married. Trust me, one day you'll find somebody and you'll fall head over heels in love and it'll be the most wonderful, incredible, fantastic thing that's ever happened to you and you'll know why we can't get married—"

He grabbed her shoulders, hugged her again and laughed. "I love you, Analise! In a sisterly way."

"You do understand! I'm so glad! Now, I know you're wondering why I've been traveling all around the countryside, and you wouldn't believe what some of the countryside outside Texas is like. Anyway, I had planned this to be a wedding present because I knew how much it meant to you, but now it's kind of an unwedding present—"

"Analise," he interrupted, moving toward the phone, "I want to hear all about your trip, but there's somebody I've got to call first, before she gets out of town."

"But Lucas, don't you want to know about this horrible woman who framed your father and ruined his life?"

Lucas stopped with his hand poised over the phone. "What did you say?"

"Nick uncovered proof that your father's innocent!" She told him the story of Abbie Prather's theft and how she'd shifted the blame to his father. But before she got a chance to tell him about Sara, he placed two fingers on her lips to silence her.

"Thank you," he said. "That's the most wonderful present anybody ever gave me and you're the best friend I've ever had. But you've got to stop talking long enough for me to make a very important phone call. I have to catch Sara before she leaves town."

Analise yanked his fingers away. "Sara? Not Sara Martin?"

"So you *were* tracking her!"

Analise lifted her hands to her cheeks. "You've met my sister?"

"Then she is your sister?"

"My twin sister! Do my parents know about her?"

"No. They—"

"Oh, good! I can surprise them! She's the reason Abbie Prather stole the money. She got Sara and—"

"Wait a minute. What do you mean, Abbie Prather got Sara? Sara was raised by a woman named June Martin."

"I'm trying to tell you if you'd quit interrupting me! Abbie Prather took the identity of June Martin after she stole that money and went to South Dakota with Sara. I can't believe you've actually met her! What do you mean you've got to catch her before she leaves town? When's she leaving? Why?"

"Tonight, right now."

"No! She can't do that! Stop dillydallying! Call her, quick! Don't let her get away!" She snatched up the phone and handed it to him.

"Analise, I love Sara. If I can catch her, I'm going to ask her to marry me."

Analise's eyes filled with tears and she hugged him again. "Oh, Lucas! That's so incredible! You're going to be my brother for real! Hurry and call her! I can't wait to meet my sister! My twin sister! Does she look exactly like me?"

"Yes, she looks exactly like you," he said, then punched in a number on the telephone keypad. "Room 112," he requested, and she heard an excitement in Lucas's voice she'd never heard before.

But then his face darkened. "Are you sure?" he asked in despair.

"Lucas, what's the matter?"

"She checked out ten minutes ago."

"Where's she going? Back to Deauxville? That's the small town in Missouri where she last lived, but you probably know that already. Don't worry. We can find her. I'll call Nick. He can find anyone. He's a brilliant detective." Her offer of Nick's services had nothing to do with how much she wanted to see him again. He *was* a brilliant detective. That's the only reason she'd suggested calling him.

"No, she's not going to Deauxville. She's going to Dallas, so she'll be taking Highway 20 West. Did you drive here in your car?"

"Of course I drove here in my car. Oh, I see! You bet we can catch her! Come on!" She pulled her keys from her bag.

Lucas moved between her and the door. "No. I have to do this myself. Can I borrow your car?"

"Oh, Lucas, you can't drive as fast as I can! I'll drive

and you look. I have to be there! I've tracked my sister all over the country, and I can't wait to meet her in person!''

He held out a hand for the keys. ''Trust me, desperation will make a race-car driver out of me. And I promise to bring Sara back as soon as I can catch her, but I have to do this one alone.''

She relinquished the keys and gave him a wide smile. ''Okay, but just remember, gas pedal on the floor, brake pedal in the air.''

Lucas charged out the door, down the sidewalk and into her little red sports car. He was, indeed, moving faster than she'd ever seen him move.

''Drive like the wind, Lucas!'' she called after him then giggled to herself at her paraphrasing of the silly cliché.

He pulled away from the house with a screeching of tires. ''Way to go, Lucas!'' she called, though he'd already rounded the corner without slowing and couldn't hear her. Her sister certainly had an effect on him.

For one wistful moment she thought how wonderful it would be if Nick loved her like that.

But he didn't and he couldn't, not when she was a disaster perpetually happening, not when all he wanted was peace and quiet and solitude, and the only thing she knew about those elements came from her dictionary.

Well, she had too many good things in her life to feel sorry for herself over the one thing she couldn't have. Right now the wound of being separated from Nick was fresh and raw and painful, but it would heal with time.

Oh, yeah? An annoying little voice taunted. *Like you healed from the loss of your sister when she was only three weeks old and you didn't even remember her?*

That's different! she told that annoying little voice. *Mind your own business!*

She went inside to call her parents, but then hesitated with her hand on the phone.

What if Lucas didn't catch Sara? She hated to get her parents' hopes up after all these years only to disappoint them. Perhaps she ought to wait until she was certain that Sara would return tonight.

In the meantime she could sit and wait.

That wasn't something she did well under ordinary circumstances, and tonight was decidedly extraordinary.

Maybe she ought to call Nick's office, see if they could locate him and have him standing by in case Lucas didn't catch Sara and they needed to find her in Dallas.

She turned away from the phone in disgust. Figuring out a flimsy pretext that would allow her to see Nick again didn't fit in with her vow to put him out of her mind.

She flopped onto Lucas's sofa. She'd sit and wait.

She drummed her fingers on the padded arm, looked around the room then checked her watch. Thirty seconds. How on earth was she going to be able to stand this waiting, this not knowing whether she was going to be meeting her sister any minute now or whether Lucas would come through the door alone?

Maybe calling Nick wouldn't be such a bad idea after all. Just in case.

Of course it was a bad idea.

She needed something to munch on…cookies, peanuts, popcorn. Automatically, she reached for her tote bag, rummaging around inside, but she'd eaten all the goodies. Not even one cheese twist remained.

Lucas rarely kept anything in his kitchen except real food, but she made a quick search anyway, turning up a bag of chocolate chips and a couple of packages of microwave popcorn. Fat-free, but it was better than nothing.

This was going to be a long wait.

However, eating would soothe her nerves and, if she kept her hands moving constantly, shoving food into her mouth, she couldn't reach for the phone to call Nick.

She didn't dare go to the store for fear of missing Lucas and Sara, but there was a recipe on the package of chocolate chips for cookies. After she finished the popcorn, maybe she could make some cookies. How hard could it be with a recipe to follow?

Nick pulled up in front of Lucas Daniels's house. Analise's car was nowhere in sight. After calling her parents and being told they were expecting her but she hadn't arrived yet, he'd been certain she'd gone straight to Lucas's, but apparently she hadn't.

She must be somewhere in Briar Creek. The way she drove, it was inconceivable she was still on the road. He'd wasted valuable time arguing with himself back in Tyler before he'd started after her, so she should have arrived at least half an hour ago. He'd have passed her on the drive here if she'd still been en route.

He sat in his car, drumming his fingers on the steering wheel, trying to decide what to do now.

Where the hell could Analise be?

A door slammed. Against the bright, starry sky, smoke billowed from somewhere inside the wooden fence that enclosed the side yard.

Nick's heartbeat accelerated. He'd found Analise.

He got out of the car as the gate burst open and Analise charged through carrying a blazing pan. She tossed it to the ground then turned and ran toward the house.

He hurried over to stomp out the fire just as she whirled around and sprayed the burning object with a stream of water...splashing water and bits of charcoal on him.

"Nick!"

The spray stopped.

"Is that you, Nick?"

He wiped the acrid-smelling gunk off his face and smiled in spite of everything. It had only been a couple of hours since he'd seen her last, but it felt like an eternity. "It's me," he said.

She dashed over to him. "Oh, dear!" She brushed the pieces of incinerated whatever off his shirt, her touch light and breezy and oh, so welcome. "I'm sorry! I didn't see you." She stopped and looked up at him. "What are you doing here?"

Her eyes reflected the stars from the night sky overhead. He clenched his hands at his sides to prevent himself from taking her into his arms and kissing her. There was a lot they had to resolve before...if...they got to that stage. "What was that?" he asked instead, indicating the still-smoking mess.

She sighed. "I was going to make some cookies, but I couldn't find a cookie sheet, so I thought if I turned that cake pan upside down, it would be fine, only then I couldn't get the oven to light—it's gas and I was afraid I'd blow the whole place up—so I put the pan on top of the stove on a burner, only I didn't have any way to tell when it got to three hundred and fifty degrees so I turned it up pretty high because three hundred and fifty degrees sounds pretty hot, and the next thing I knew, the cookies had run down the side of the pan and the whole thing was on fire."

She was babbling. That meant she was nervous.

Oh, he knew her so well!

"Relax," he said, taking her hand in his. The touch of her slim fingers dispelled the soggy feel of his clothes against his body, the scent of smoke and burned cookies...dispelled everything except Analise's touch, Analise in the starlight.

As he held her hand, she quietened, calmed. "What are you doing here?" she repeated. "I didn't think I'd ever see you again. How did you know where Lucas lives?"

He grinned. "I'm a detective, remember?"

"Oh." She looked at him curiously, too polite to ask a

third time why he was there. "Come inside and I'll try to get some of that mess off your clothes. No wonder they never serve chocolate-chip cookies flambé. Those chips get pretty nasty when they catch fire."

She turned to go back to the house, but he took her arm. "No, wait. I need to talk to you. Out here." *Not inside with Lucas.*

"Okay." Her reply was soft, like the night air that wrapped around them, as though she sensed that what he had to say was important.

She knew him so well.

He cleared his throat. "You can't marry Lucas."

"I know," she said in that same soft voice.

He dropped her arm. "You do?"

"Well, of course I do. I figured that out a couple of days ago. I'm flaky, not stupid. I can't marry Lucas because I love him. Not like you're supposed to love somebody you marry but like a friend who deserves a wife who loves him the right way."

"If you already knew all that, why didn't you tell me?"

She looked down at the cremated cookies. "Why should I? So you could add my failed engagement to your list of Analise's Blunders? I think that list is probably long enough already and still growing."

"Does Lucas know yet?"

"Of course not. That's why I brought them outside."

"What? Oh, no, I don't mean does he know about the cookies. Does he know you're not going to marry him? Have you told him yet?"

"Sure I told him. Or he told me. I'm not sure who told who first, but it got told, so you can stop trying to take care of me. I'm not a child like your sisters were and I'm not a flake like your ex-wife. I may not do things strictly according to directions, but I manage to muddle through."

"Then—"

"There's Lucas!" Two cars turned the corner and moved down the street toward them. Analise's car followed by a midsize sedan. "Look!" Analise pointed. "He found her! Quick! Help me get this in the house so Sara won't see it! I don't want my sister's first impression of me to be my latest catastrophe!"

She snatched up the pan and ran back into the side yard.

Nick followed, trying to keep up with her steps and catch up with her conversation. "You mean Lucas isn't in the house?"

"No, he took my car to go after Sara. He's going to marry her and bring her to meet me." She ran through a patio door and into a kitchen that was going to smell like burned cookies for some time no matter how well she hid the physical evidence. "Actually, he's going to bring her to meet me before he marries her. I don't think they can get married that fast. I hope not, because I want to be her maid of honor. Or maybe Lucas's best man. Woman. Whatever."

She opened a drawer and pulled out a trash bag. "Would you put this mess in here and tie it really tight and set it on the patio? I've got to call Mom and Dad and tell them to come over to meet Sara!"

She darted from the room, leaving Nick holding the ruined pan of charcoal cookies and a plastic bag.

God, he loved that woman!

Analise darted into the living room, ran to the phone and snatched it up. "Nick, what's my parents' phone number? I'm so nervous, I can't remember my own phone number!" Thank goodness Nick was there…even though he'd apparently only come to be sure she did the right thing by Lucas. She was suddenly terrified to meet her sister, but just the knowledge that Nick was in the same house gave her courage.

He emerged from the kitchen and told her the number for her parents. With shaky fingers, she punched it in.

"Analise!" her mother exclaimed. "Where are you? What's going on?"

"I'm at Lucas's house. You and Dad need to come over right away. Don't even stop for red lights. Okay, maybe you should stop for red lights because you absolutely cannot have a wreck on the way over, but when you stop, if there's no traffic, go on through! Drive as fast as you can! Pretend you're me! This is the most important thing that's ever happened to us! Hurry!"

Without giving her mother a chance to protest, she hung up, ran to give Nick a hug and dashed outside.

Lucas and Sara were just starting up the walk, his arm around her.

Analise ran to meet them. "Is that my sister? Is that you, Sara? Omigosh, I can't believe this!" Analise enveloped Sara in an exuberant hug, then drew back to look at her. "This is unreal! You look just like me only prettier."

Sara's eyes misted with tears. She reached up and touched Analise's cheek. "My sister," she said, her voice full of wonder.

Analise nodded, tears threatening to spill from her own eyes. "I always knew you were out there. I even have a doll named Sara."

Sara laughed. "I know. I had a doll named Analise."

"I know!" Analise hooked her arm through Sara's. "We have so many years to make up for! Come inside so we can talk. I called Mom and Dad, and they're on their way over."

Sara stopped, pulling Analise up short. "Analise, do you know about our real parents?"

"Yes," she said, and for the first time it occurred to her that Sara hadn't discovered the truth yet. "I know about our real parents. You mean you don't?"

"No, I don't, and it doesn't matter anymore. I have all the family I need. Lucas and I are getting married and I've found my sister."

Analise hugged her again. "Oh, Sara, I'm so sorry you had to go through all that bad stuff, but from now on, everything's going to be wonderful! I promise!"

As they stepped onto the front porch, Nick appeared in the lighted doorway.

"That's Nick!" Analise exclaimed. "Oh, my sweet sister Sara! Have I ever got a story to tell you! Come on inside!"

She rushed past Nick and ran to get her bag. "I brought this to you." She pulled out the battered doll.

Sara lifted her hands to her cheeks, her eyes wide. "It's Analise! Where did you find her?"

"Nick found her in the attic of your house in Minnesota."

Tears streamed from Sara's eyes as she crossed the room to take the doll.

"Analise!"

Analise looked up at the sound of her mother's voice. Clare and Ralph stood in the doorway, shock evident on both their faces.

Sara stiffened. "Oh dear." Her voice was filled with distress as she turned to the older couple. "I can explain. I never meant to deceive you. I'm so sorry."

"Deceive them?" Analise repeated. "What are you talking about?"

"I let them think I was you, that I was their daughter."

"But you are! This is your mother and father. Our mother and father. Mom and Dad, meet your other daughter."

Clare Brewster's face went ghostly pale as she pressed a hand to her heart and sagged against her husband. "Annabel?" she whispered.

Sara's gaze darted from Analise to Ralph and Clare then back again, her eyes wide with confusion. Lucas moved over to stand beside her and wrap a protective arm around her. "What's going on?" he asked.

"Yes, Mom, this is Annabel except she's Sara now," Analise explained. "And, personally, I like that better than Annabel." She didn't want her parents trying to change Sara's name at this stage of her life. She had enough adapting to do without that.

Ralph held Clare tightly, and Analise wasn't sure who was supporting who. "Omigod, Clare, it's our baby!" For the first time, Analise saw tears streaking down her father's strong face.

"I don't understand." Sara's voice came out choked, barely audible, as her gaze darted back and forth between Analise and the older couple.

Clare stepped forward and touched Sara's hair, her expression one of awe as she looked from one daughter to the other. "Annabel? Is it really you?"

Ralph approached tentatively and took Sara's face between his hands, his gaze scanning her features. "It is, Mother. It's our Annabel." His voice was soft and full of wonder. "It was you at the house this past week, not Analise, wasn't it?"

Sara nodded, the movement jerky and uncertain. "That was me." Confusion still reigned in her eyes, but Analise could see a glimmer of hope, like the first rays of dawn.

Ralph brushed Sara's hair back from her face, his big hands gentle, and smiled. "I could always tell the difference, even when you were babies. I knew something wasn't quite right last week, but it never entered my mind that you'd come back. We never thought we'd see you again. This is a miracle."

Sara swallowed hard. "My real parents?" She looked at Analise as if for confirmation. "They're my real parents?"

"Yes, they are. It's a long story, but we've got the rest of our lives to talk about it. June Martin kidnapped you."

"Kidnapped?" Sara shot Lucas a quick glance over her shoulder. "That's why she kept moving, why she was so scared somebody was going to take me away from her? She was afraid my real parents would find me?"

"We tried," Clare said, tears of joy flowing freely past her wide smile as she took Sara's hands. "We tried for years and couldn't find a trace so we finally had to give up. But we never stopped loving you and missing you."

A hesitant smile spread over Sara's face. "You really are my mother and father?"

"Yes, sweetheart. We really are." Clare opened her arms and Sara fell into them, laughing and sobbing.

"I wanted you to be! I was so envious that Analise had you for parents and I hated myself for that envy! But I have you, too!"

Ralph pulled Analise to him, then wrapped his arms around the three of them. "I never thought the day would come when I'd have all my girls together again. Your mother never wanted to give up. I made her because it was killing her to hope. But she was right all along!"

"I always knew you were out there somewhere," Clare said.

"Me, too," Analise said. "My heart knew."

Entangled in the group hug of her family, Analise chastised herself because she couldn't feel one hundred percent happy. She'd found her twin sister, her best friend was going to be her brother, she realized that her parents hadn't doubted her because they thought she was a ditz but because they'd feared for her safety…but still there was an empty spot. Still, greedy girl that she was, she wanted it all, wanted the one person who could fill that empty spot…wanted Nick.

She peered around to where he stood behind them. He

smiled and gave her a thumbs-up sign. Obviously he thought he'd done the job she'd hired him to do. Nothing personal. Everything was complete for him. He could leave now.

She separated herself from the group. "I'll be right back," she promised. Her parents and Sara had plenty to discuss for a few minutes.

She needed to talk to Nick, release him and let him be on his way. Knowing how he felt about families, she was sure all this reunion stuff was bound to be making him uncomfortable.

Chapter Thirteen

Nick stood in a spraddle-legged stance, arms folded across his chest. He looked sturdy and magnificent and something else, something that flickered only briefly in his steady gaze and then was gone. Wistfulness?

Nah. He'd probably gotten chocolate-chip cookie ashes in his eyes.

"Thank you," she said. "Without you, this wouldn't be happening."

He smiled. "Yes, it would have. If you'd never left home, Sara would have found you."

"Oh. Well, that's true. But I might be marrying Lucas instead of her." *And never have known what love really is with all its heights and depths. Never have had my heart broken.*

"Do you really think you would have married him?"

She looked back to where her dear friend stood gazing down at her sister with love in his eyes while Sara explained they were getting married. She smiled and shook her head. "No. I could never have married him. That's the real reason I ran away. I knew it all along, but I didn't want to face disappointing my parents again.''

Lucas spotted her looking at him, leaned over to say something to Sara, and everyone turned toward Analise and Nick. Lucas strode over and extended his hand. "I'm Lucas Daniels. You must be Nick."

Oh, dear! Analise searched her mind frantically, trying to remember what she'd told Lucas about Nick. She'd tried to be so careful not to say anything that would give her away, but Lucas knew her so well. It was terrible to have a friend so close he could read her mind...and her heart.

"This is Nick Claiborne," Analise said, introducing him to her curious family. "He's the detective I hired to find proof of Lucas's father's innocence, and along the way we found Sara."

Sara, Ralph and Clare came over to shake hands with Nick and ask questions about Lucas's father, about June Martin, Sara, Nick's travels with Analise. He handled the melee quite graciously, but Analise knew he must be getting antsy in the presence of her rowdy family. He was doubtless anxious to get back to peace and sanity and solitude.

Finally Lucas and Sara disappeared into the kitchen to get some tea for everyone, and Analise took advantage of the slight break to rescue Nick.

As Clare and Ralph urged him toward a chair, she took his arm. "Nick's had a long day, Mom. I'm going to walk him to his car and then I'll be right back." *I'm just going to leave my heart lying out on the curb and bring the rest of me right back. No big deal.*

Instead of gratitude in Nick's eyes, she caught a fleeting glimpse of something else, something indiscernible.

Regret?

Couldn't be. It was only a reflection of her own regret. Or more chocolate-chip-cookie ashes.

He said goodbye to her parents, then called out farewells to Sara and Lucas in the kitchen while she waited, her smile wearing very thin.

Leading Nick out of the house and out of her life was one of the hardest things she'd ever done, and he wasn't making it any easier, drawing it out, playing the part of a guest who hated to leave.

Finally they walked out into the summer night.

"Sorry about all the chaos," she said.

"I kind of enjoyed it. I don't usually get to see the end results of my work. It was nice to see everybody so happy."

She started down the porch steps, but Nick stopped at the edge and drew in a deep breath. "Smells wonderful out here. Honeysuckle."

"Does it? I hadn't noticed."

The moonless night was dark, and the light spilling from Lucas's living room only made it harder to see Nick's face as he looked down at her. His features were craggy and shadowed, and at first she thought his movement toward her was a trick of those shadows.

Then his hand cupped her face and his lips brushed hers…tentatively?

Nick wasn't tentative about anything.

Was he?

His lips returned to hers, more confident this time, and the night exploded around her, alive with the scents of honeysuckle and roses and Nick, the sounds of crickets and katydids, the feel of a warm breeze on her skin, Nick's fingers on her cheek, her heart thudding against her ribs…and Nick's lips on hers. Reveling in the moment, she savored every heightened sensation.

Too soon he pulled away and laid his forehead against hers. "Analise," he murmured, "what would you think about you and me getting harried, too?"

She scowled and pushed away. "Harried? Is that your special euphemism for sex? Are you trying to say you think I'd make a mess of that, too? That's not funny, Nick Claiborne! You can just get in your car and drive to your plane and fly off into the sky all alone and then nobody will be able to harry you!"

His widening smile didn't make her feel any better. She'd never have suspected him of being mean. She jerked her arm away when he tried to take it.

"Analise, I didn't say *harried*. I said *married*. I've been trying to say it for over an hour now."

She turned back to him. "Married? You and me?"

"Yes, you and me. Who else? We're the only people out here."

For one brief, ecstatic moment she considered it. Married to Nick. Coming home to him every night. Kissing him...and more...every night.

But he'd only asked her to marry him. He hadn't said he loved her. He'd been married once to a woman he hadn't loved, had only felt obligated to care for. Just as she couldn't marry Lucas because she didn't love him in the right way, so she couldn't agree to marry Nick because she did love him in the right way...wildly, passionately, with every ounce of her unpredictable being. "So you can take care of me and get me out of jail?"

He sighed and ran a hand through his hair. "Analise Brewster, you are absolutely the most exasperating woman I have ever proposed to."

"Oh? And just how many women have you proposed to?"

"Counting you, one. Kay asked me to marry her. But I have a feeling you'd still rank as the most exasperating if there'd been a dozen." He took her hand, and she let him this time. "Analise, you do have a talent for getting into situations that most people could never even imagine. But

I've seen you use that same ability to get yourself out. Granted, your methods are a little unusual, but they always seem to work. You don't need a keeper, and I'm not applying for the job even if you did. I want to marry you because I love you.''

"You do?" Her heart lurched into a series of handsprings even as her mind couldn't quite accept what he said.

"Of course I do. With all my heart.''

"But I make you crazy.''

"That's true. I do get a little upset with you sometimes.''

"Sometimes? Hah! On a regular basis.''

"Maybe. But that's only—well, mostly...partly—because you've made me reassess my whole life. Until you came along, I kept myself locked away. I thought the only way I could be safe was to be alone, not get emotionally involved, keep at arm's length from everybody. When my sisters left, I wasn't happy to get back my solitude after all. I was devastated because they'd left me. I married Kay, but that didn't fill the emptiness. When she left, I made up my mind to insulate myself from all those treacherous emotions, never to get involved again. I thought I had my life all neatly and safely laid out.'' He drew one finger along her cheek and down her throat. "And then you came along and changed everything. You taught me about being brave enough to love and risk losing. You taught me that love goes on whether the people who love each other are together physically or not.''

"I taught you all that? Are you sure you have the right person? I thought the only thing I taught you is that you have to wash your hands with soap and water immediately after applying tanning cream.''

He cringed. "Yes, I'll never forget that lesson. But this morning when I found out I'm an uncle, everything started to come together.''

"Sharon had her baby? That's great! Boy or girl?''

"A girl. They named her Nicole Renee, and Sharon was very upset that I wasn't there."

"Of course she was! What did you expect?"

"I didn't expect her to need me, but she did. All day I thought about her and about what you said, that we don't stop loving someone just because we start loving someone new. Then I got back to Tyler and talked to Ben and he told me about Sara's kidnapping. I knew then why you'd been so persistent about finding her. You've loved her for years without even remembering her except in your heart."

She should resist the urge to say "I told you so." But she couldn't. "I've been trying to tell you that for some time."

"Yes, you have. I didn't believe you. After I drove away from you at the airport this afternoon, I couldn't stop thinking about the ecstatic look on your face when I told you about Sara. I was in my driveway when I finally admitted to myself that you were right and that it was my fault I'd lost touch with my family. Sure, they're the ones who left home, but I could have flown to see them anytime. I let them walk out of my life. Kay, too. She knew I didn't love her the way I should. It was my choice. You were strong enough not to do that. You kept looking for Sara no matter what obstacles you faced, even a cranky detective."

"And flying through a storm. Don't forget the storm. I certainly never will."

"Flying through a storm when you're afraid of flying. I decided to take a lesson from you and not let that happen to me again. I backed out of that driveway and tracked you down. I was...and am...determined to make every effort to see that another woman I love doesn't walk out of my life."

"Me?" she whispered. "You don't want me to walk out of your life?"

"You. I made up my mind to fight for you, to tell you all the reasons you can't marry Lucas. But you already knew them. So now all I have to do is convince you why you should marry me.''

The idea tugged at her, promising a lifetime of thrills at her fingertips, of waking in the morning to find Nick beside her, of feeling his lips on hers with all the explosive fireworks that action generated.

''I can tell you why I *shouldn't* marry you,'' she said reluctantly.

''Because you don't love me.''

''Don't be dumb. Of course I love you. If I didn't love you quite so much, I maybe could marry you.''

''Analise, that doesn't make any sense whatsoever. I have to admit, most of the things you come up with have their own brand of illogical logic, but not that. If you love me as much as I love you, why shouldn't we get married?''

''Don't you remember what else I said? Once I get all impassioned about something, once my adrenaline starts flowing, that's when things go wrong. My brain disconnects, and I do really dumb stuff and...chaos. And I'm certainly all impassioned about you! Our marriage would be complete chaos!''

He curled one finger under her chin, tilting her head to look at him. ''Wonderful chaos. I'm counting on it. Though you seem to be forgetting that you don't have to prove anything anymore. You can stop trying so hard. All your parents were ever worried about was losing you the way they lost Sara.''

''You're saying I can skip the skydiving classes.''

''I think so.'' He leaned forward and brushed her lips with his, the kiss as light as the brush of butterfly wings, yet it sent her blood rushing, her heart pounding, her adrenaline surging.

''It might cause fewer problems if I got all my thrills at home,'' she whispered.

''Is that a *yes?*''

"I guess if you're brave enough to try it, well, so am I."

"Like I told you, real bravery means you do it even if you're scared."

As his lips claimed hers, she'd never felt less frightened. The future spread around them like the wide Texas sky sprinkled with stars. She had nothing to prove because Nick loved her just the way she was.

Epilogue

The attendants trailed slowly down the aisle of the Grand Avenue Methodist Church and stood alongside Nick and Lucas then turned to look toward the back of the church where Analise clutched her sister's hand in a death grip.

"You're not nervous, are you?" Sara whispered.

"No, of course not." But it was hard for Analise to lie to her twin. "Yes! Aren't you?"

"A little. But it's a good kind of nervous."

When the last attendant was in place, the minister looked at the organist and lifted a restraining hand. "Ladies and gentlemen," he addressed the standing-room-only crowd in the church, "you've been invited here today to share the exchanging of vows between Analise Brewster and Lucas Daniels. As many of you already know, there's been a slight change in the program. Analise and Lucas will still be exchanging vows, but not with each other. Analise will be marrying Nick Claiborne—" he indicated the groom on his left "—and Lucas—" he turned to the groom on his right "—will marry Analise's twin sister, Sara Brewster."

He nodded to the organist who began to play the wedding march.

Analise took one of her father's arms and Sara took the other. In identical white satin gowns they walked down the aisle toward their grooms.

As they passed their mother, Clare smiled as happy tears streaked down her face.

"Who gives these women in marriage?" the minister asked.

"Their mother and I," Ralph said, beaming proudly at each daughter as he relinquished her to her future husband.

Analise still couldn't believe her quest for a wedding gift for Lucas had brought her Nick.

She exchanged vows with Nick, and Sara exchanged vows with Lucas. As Analise slipped the ring on her husband's finger, she looked into his eyes and knew the real gift was love, and they'd all received that in abundance.

* * * * *

Be sure to look for the next book
from Sally Carleen.
Don't miss THE PRINCE'S HEIR,
available in October
from Silhouette Romance.

If you enjoyed what you just read,
then we've got an offer you can't resist!

Take 2 bestselling love stories FREE!
Plus get a FREE surprise gift!

Clip this page and mail it to Silhouette Reader Service™

IN U.S.A.	IN CANADA
3010 Walden Ave.	P.O. Box 609
P.O. Box 1867	Fort Erie, Ontario
Buffalo, N.Y. 14240-1867	L2A 5X3

YES! Please send me 2 free Silhouette Romance® novels and my free surprise gift. Then send me 6 brand-new novels every month, which I will receive months before they're available in stores. In the U.S.A., bill me at the bargain price of $2.90 plus 25¢ delivery per book and applicable sales tax, if any*. In Canada, bill me at the bargain price of $3.25 plus 25¢ delivery per book and applicable taxes**. That's the complete price and a savings of over 10% off the cover prices—what a great deal! I understand that accepting the 2 free books and gift places me under no obligation ever to buy any books. I can always return a shipment and cancel at any time. Even if I never buy another book from Silhouette, the 2 free books and gift are mine to keep forever. So why not take us up on our invitation. You'll be glad you did!

215 SEN CNE7
315 SEN CNE9

Name	(PLEASE PRINT)	
Address	Apt.#	
City	State/Prov.	Zip/Postal Code

* Terms and prices subject to change without notice. Sales tax applicable in N.Y.
** Canadian residents will be charged applicable provincial taxes and GST.
  All orders subject to approval. Offer limited to one per household.
  ® are registered trademarks of Harlequin Enterprises Limited.

SROM99   ©1998 Harlequin Enterprises Limited

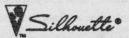